Praise for *Gone to Pot*:

"Jess is the feisty, funny, opinionated, can't-keep-her-down-for-long 'crone' we all hope to become. In this rollicking tale of desperate ingenuity, Jess shows us that you're never too old to grow."

—Anne DeGrace, author of *Flying with Amelia*

"Jennifer Craig's 'Jess' is a lot like her; a wicked Yorkshire lass whose pluck and humor pack trouble into an old kit bag, and this time the bag is bursting with green. Survival of an old crone at her best."

—Rita Moir, author of *The Third Crop*

"When the going gets tough, the tough get growing. In Jess, the unsinkable centerpiece of Gone to Pot, *Jennifer Craig has given us a mother, grandmother, friend, and citizen who is memorable for her humor, resilience, practicality, and irreverence, to say nothing of her green thumb and dab hand with grow lights. It's a funny novel, and a tender one, that will make you think twice about the possibilities of your basement and will also make you want to visit Nelson, the jewel of the Kootenays, which is lovingly described. I hope we'll hear more about Jess and her gang. She won't be going gentle any time soon into any good night, that's for sure."*

—Bill Richardson, author of *The First Little Bastard to Call Me Gramps: Poems of the Late Middle Ages*

GONE TO POT

a novel

Gone to Pot

JENNIFER CRAIG

Second Story Press

Library and Archives Canada Cataloguing in Publication

Craig, Jennifer, 1934-, author
Gone to pot / by Jennifer Craig.

Issued in print and electronic formats.
ISBN 978-1-77260-034-6 (paperback).
—ISBN 978-1-77260-035-3 (epub)

I. Title.

PS8605.R346G66 2017   C813'.6   C2016-906966-4

C2016-906967-2

Cover: © Greg Stevenson, i2iart.com
Editors: Carolyn Jackson, Kathryn Cole
Design: Melissa Kaita

Printed and bound in Canada

*Second Story Press gratefully acknowledges the support of the
Ontario Arts Council and the Canada Council for the Arts for our
publishing program. We acknowledge the financial support of the
Government of Canada through the Canada Book Fund.*

ONTARIO ARTS COUNCIL
CONSEIL DES ARTS DE L'ONTARIO
an Ontario government agency
un organisme du gouvernement de l'Ontario

Canada Council   Conseil des Arts
for the Arts   du Canada

Funded by the Government of Canada
Financé par le gouvernement du Canada | Canadä

Published by
SECOND STORY PRESS
20 Maud Street, Suite 401
Toronto, ON M5V 2M5
www.secondstorypress.ca

For Auntie Von

1

BLOODY HELL, I've gone and done it now. I lay in a crumpled heap between a thicket of flower pots, my head cushioned in a marijuana plant, staring up into a 1000-watt light bulb. I struggled to get up. My loose shirt had caught in the pallet that supported the pots—and now me. The more I struggled the tighter the shirt pulled around my throat. Was this to be my end? Either throttled by a shirt or roasted to a crisp by a grow light?

How did I get into this mess? Two things started it: the fire at the Grizzly Grill; and news of the stock market slump. Crash and burn is how my troubles began.

My workplace, the Grizzly Grill on Baker Street, was within walking distance of my house. I enjoyed the walk down the tree-lined street, past the lovely old stone church, but that day everything was gray—the grass, the bushes, the trees—all coated with winter gravel and dust. Patches of ice still lingered ready to topple the unwary. How nice it would be to get out of Nelson, to go somewhere warm with palm trees and greenery, to lie in a deck chair with nothing to worry about. But holidays were not for me. Not then. Not ever.

A fire truck sirened past me. Nearly deafened me, it did. Mind you, with the fire hall just round the corner and the hospital just up the road, hearing sirens where I lived was not unusual. People came out of their houses and began running down the hill. Like a fool I joined them. Why? I don't usually follow the herd or run on an icy path, or even a clear path, for that matter.

Then I saw the smoke. A huge ball of black poured out from somewhere on Baker Street and rolled upward and toward us. I ran faster.

Next thing I was sprawled on the sidewalk. *Daft bugger, you should know better than to try to run at all, let alone downhill.* A couple of youngsters helped me up and I sat on a wall to get my breath and assess the damage. The young man with his baseball cap on backwards kneeled down to look at my leg. We rolled up my pant leg and watched the knee swell.

"I'll be okay," I told him. "I'll just sit a minute. You go ahead."

"You're sure?"

I nodded. He stood up to leave, walked a few steps and then turned to call out, "Your skateboard's under that car."

A good laugh always helps. My gammy knee stiffened up and let me know it was having none of it. One grazed hand dropped blood on the sidewalk. I found a tissue in my apron, pressed it on the graze, and then stood up. My pants were covered in gravel. Would it be better to go to work like that or go back home to change and be late? I dithered for a minute and then carried on.

Limping, I managed to reach the back of the crowd standing in silence at a police barrier. I watched the Grizzly Grill go up in flames from a safe distance. There go my comfy loafers that I got from the thrift shop for five bucks. I would be on the dole now—at my age—but I fretted more over those loafers than my future. They didn't pinch my bunions like my other shoes.

Dense smoke made it difficult to see where it was coming from. The smell was terrible, like singed hair, and a roaring noise, like a waterfall, filled the street. The fire truck had its ladder up and from it a firefighter directed a jet of water into the smoke. He looked so tiny in his yellow uniform and helmet standing on top of the ladder, like the toy I gave my grandson.

I'm not a gawker and my knee hurt, so I began to push my way out of the crowd. "Hey, Jess," I heard someone say. I turned to see Swan, another waitress at the Grill. "Looks like we're out of work."

"Has it completely gone?" I asked her. "What happened?"

"Word on Twitter that it started in the basement." Swan looked up from her cell phone. "Electrical they think."

"Thank goodness it wasn't open yet," I said. "So no one but Joe would be there." Joe was our cook and he would have started work earlier, setting up the kitchen and prepping food and all that. "Is he all right?"

"Dunno. I just got here." Swan looked at me briefly through her heavy mascara as she continued to text.

"I might as well go home. But I'll wait until I know if Joe is okay." I turned around. "I have to sit down. I fell and my knee is killing me."

"Go sit on that bench. I'll see if I can find Joe." Swan helped me to one of the benches set in an alcove of low, stone walls. "Back in a flash."

Swan had only been on the job about three weeks and was still wet behind the ears. She was a bit daft—sashaying around the Grill like a princess, standing beside a customer's table with one hip stuck out as if she needed a replacement. She could never remember what the specials were. Waitressing doesn't give much time for conversation, so I didn't know her very well.

I sat, with my knee throbbing, and watched the backs of people all staring at the fire and the firefighters. A policeman in a yellow jacket and bicycle helmet held the crowd behind a barricade and another manned the next junction directing traffic. An ambulance parked on the cross street didn't seem to be busy, thank goodness.

One section of the crowd stopped staring down the street as its attention turned to a heavily built woman made even bulkier by a puffy black jacket crowned with a felt fedora-style hat. She waved her arms and shouted, "Behold, the Lord has visited this fire upon you because of your sinful natures. Repent! Repent now before the whole town burns. Turn to Jesus for redemption. Find your path back to—"

She stopped yelling as a young woman in a red toque shook her fist at her. "Shut up you righteous nutcase. Go back to your cage."

The proselyte took a couple of steps toward Red Toque and pointed her finger. "Sinner," she shouted, "repent your evil ways before the town burns before your eyes!"

I cheered for Red Toque as the two women faced off.

Jesus freaks always got up my nose with their holier-than-thou attitude. The policeman with the bicycle approached them. I couldn't hear what they were saying, but there was a lot of arm waving before Fedora Hat strode away up the hill, her challenger rejoined the crowd, and the policeman returned to his position.

A tall, gangly young man suddenly appeared and came over to sit on my bench. He didn't look at me as he plonked himself down, sat with splayed legs, and stared into space with the kind of dark brown eyes you see in Middle Eastern men. Although he wore a black toque, the sort that's associated with bank robbers, he wasn't at all threatening. In fact, he seemed quite gentle with his one earring and one of those little bits of beard they call a soul patch.

After a while he leaned back and lifted his left wrist as if to read a watch. Then he shook his head slightly when he saw his bare arm and asked, "Got the time?"

"Twenty to twelve," I said.

He went on staring into space as I looked around for Swan. A few moments later she appeared. "Oh hey, Marcus, there you are. Jess, this is Marcus."

She sat down between the young man and me. Marcus stood up and hovered awkwardly before squatting on the wall to one side of us. "Joe's okay," Swan said. "They've taken him to hospital to check him out. He's the one who sounded the alarm."

"Oh good," I said. "One less thing to worry about."

"Marcus and I are going to Oso for a Java. Wanna join us?"

I limped up the hill behind them. My knee was hurting

badly, but I could still hobble. After a block, Swan looked around to see where I was, and then stopped to wait. She wore an enormous knitted poncho in light brown wool with dark green leaves embroidered on it and from a distance I got the impression that a giant cactus was waiting for me. The poncho swirled over her usual waitress outfit—black jeans and a sweater that showed a layer of her undershirt. That was the fashion, yes, but it looked as if the sweater had shrunk. Why did youngsters want to show their underwear? In my young day, we did our best to hide it. She took my arm and her support helped me the rest of the way.

Marcus walked on with a gait like a colt that couldn't control its legs. When Swan and I got to Oso Negro's, he was at the front of the line ready to order our coffees. The place was packed, probably because it was out of range of the smoke. Swan quickly positioned herself so that as soon as a group looked as if it was about to leave, she could grab the table. I waited with Marcus to help him carry our coffees and his muffin.

"Well done," I said to Swan once we all sat down at the table she'd secured.

Marcus put down the cups with hands as big as a gorilla's, and as hairy. He pulled off his toque to reveal short blond hair that seemed surprising given his dark eyes and complexion. Fair hair and brown eyes are most attractive, and I couldn't stop staring at him.

So far I hadn't heard him speak other than asking the time. It looked as though I was to be kept wondering when Swan turned to me and said, "Well, Jess, now you're not working, whatcha gonna do?"

"I don't know. Look for a job, I suppose. What will you do?"

Swan gazed into the distance as she played with the one long strand of hair she had on her head, dyed purple to contrast with her otherwise short black stubble. "Maybe try for a job as a doctor's receptionist. Or a dentist's."

With the ring though her lip, her eyes so heavy with makeup that you could hardly see them, and her extraordinary hair arrangement—you couldn't call it a 'hair do' as she hardly had any—she'd frighten patients half to death.

"You'd be good at that," I said trying to be encouraging. I turned to Marcus who was sitting staring into his coffee cup as if it would reveal his fortune. "What do you do, Marcus?"

He looked up with expressionless eyes. "Not much," he managed to utter in a deep, husky voice. "Odd jobs. You know."

"What sort of odd jobs?" I persisted.

He looked puzzled.

"Marcus is a total MacGyver," Swan said, coming to his rescue. "He's a whiz with electrical stuff."

"Oh. What do you think started the fire?"

Marcus grunted "Dunno," and carried on staring into his cup. Normally I get on well with young men—in fact, better than with men of my own age—but this one was conversationally deficient.

"Do you two live together?" I asked.

Swan laughed. "No, I share an apartment with a girlfriend," she said. "But I help Marcus out quite a bit. What sort of job will you look for, Jess?"

"I started training as a nurse," I said. Then added, "In

the olden days. Then I got rheumatic fever. It left me with a dickey heart and I had to stop training. But I've worked as an aide in nursing homes, so I might look for a job as a caregiver. Someone's elderly relative perhaps."

"Does it pay much?" Swan said.

"Not as well as a waitress with the tips." I didn't tell her it was a lousy job and the last thing I wanted. Sick people leading a purposeless life can be very demanding, and I'd be no better than a servant. Jess, fetch this. Jess, close the window. Jess, take dear Tubby Wubby for his walkies. No thank you.

"You could just retire, right?"

"I wish I could, but I can't afford to."

"Don't you own a house?"

"Yes, but that's all I own. No pension or any income." I enjoyed the attention Swan paid me. I don't see much of young people outside of work. Marcus just sat and brooded as though we weren't present.

"Well it's one more house than I own." Swan laughed.

"We were lucky. My husband and I built a house in Vancouver before prices skyrocketed. So I was able to buy a house here when we split up."

"You could take in renters. Lots of students looking for rooms in this town."

"That's a great idea. I'll think about it." I had thought about it, but I'd once had a stranger living in the house and I hated it. Fine when you're young, but you get set in your ways at my age. I'm quite frugal, like most Yorkshire folk, and when my lodger put on the washing machine for two pairs of panties and a pair of tights, I went spare. I showed her how to hand wash—dramatically. She left.

I liked solitude after being with people all day, and I certainly didn't want to wait on someone at home or cater to their needs or have the television blaring nonstop. Just hearing someone else moving about in my home put me on edge. But I might have to end up renting a room if I couldn't get a job.

"Well if you do decide to rent out, let me know. I can spread the word." Swan leaned across the table and helped herself to a piece of Marcus's muffin.

"Thanks." I sipped my coffee and looked around. "I wonder if they're hiring people here?" Everyone behind the counter could still be in school so I wouldn't be eligible, but Swan might.

"No chance. I inquired. There's a waiting list," Swan said.

Swan asked if I'd be okay getting home and I thanked her and said it was only a couple of blocks and I'd take it slowly. We parted with promises to keep in touch, but I doubted this would happen. We had very little in common apart from being unemployed waitresses, and most of the time I didn't understand a word she said. Nor did I shave off half my hair or stick metal in my nose.

I plodded up the hill to my house. A car's bumper sticker caught my eye. 'Shit Happens.' "You can say that again," I said to a startled young man as he emerged from the church food bank. He looked at the bumper, then grinned. "Right."

The food bank. I had only seen it as a place to contribute—what would it be like to have to go in there? When I was younger and married and had more money, I volunteered in Vancouver's downtown east side, working with drug addicts, people with mental health problems, lost souls, and plain old poverty victims. These were the sort of people who used food banks. Not me. What would it be like to be hungry all the time or to live as a bundle of clothing in a cardboard box or not to have a daily shower? The thought of ending up like that in my old age—well bugger that for a lark. Not while I had my wits. I could always find a job.

The phone rang as soon as I got in. "Mum, are you okay?" Jason said. "I just heard that the Grill went up in flames."

"I'm fine, luv."

"Thank goodness. I was really worried when I heard, though they did say no one was hurt."

"I hadn't arrived when it happened. Good thing it wasn't half an hour later. Did you hear how it started?"

"Something electrical in the basement, they said on the news. What are you going to do now?"

"Look for a job, I suppose."

"Why don't you come for dinner? We can talk after the kids are in bed. You know they'd love to see you."

"That would be nice."

I put the kettle on and went upstairs to change. I liked to look neat at work so I wore tailored black pants, a smart shirt and a short black apron with a large pocket. And flat comfy loafers, of course, that I left at the café. My work clothes went into the laundry basket and I pulled on loose pants and a sweatshirt that were anything but smart. I fished out my Edwardian cameo brooch, the only valuable thing I own, and hung it round my neck from its ribbon. I believe in using things, not hiding them away in safe places. Like most cameos mine had a carving of a woman's head, the woman representing Ceres, the goddess of the harvest. It's my good luck charm. My grandmother left it to me. I rubbed it and called on Ceres to bring me abundance—abundance of anything, but money in particular.

I decided to soak in a bath, something I rarely did, especially in the middle of the day. Mainly because once I got my body into a bathtub, it was a helluva job to get it out again. But the idea seemed deliciously wicked. I needed to have a good think and my knee would like a rest in nice, warm water. At the back of the bathroom cupboard I found a bottle of bubble bath someone had given me for Christmas two years before. I turned the tap to Hot. A squirt of rusty water came out. Then to Cold. Fine: clear water. Back to Hot—and more rusty muck.

I pulled on my sweats again and went down to the basement. On the bottom step I was safe from the pool of water that would have made a duck happy. "That tank wasn't even ten years old," I muttered as I waded across to turn off the water and the gas. How much did bloody hot water tanks cost? That would take care of my holiday pay.

I slopped upstairs to have a cup of tea and turn on the radio. The news relayed the information that the Dow Jones Industrial index had fallen by some horrifying percentage, resulting in the collapse of many companies. "*When it comes to wealth suddenly disappearing, the stock market can be diabolically frightful,*" the newscaster said. "*Usually this happens in October, but not this year. This year it's February with its Black Tuesday.*"

Serve the greedy buggers right. That's what you get when you care more about dollars than people. The amount of money some people made by doing nothing was…what's the word, obscene. Oh bugger—what about Nordwall Enterprises?

"Safe as houses" my financial advisor had said. "By the time you're ready to retire, you'll have a nice little profit that will yield a comfortable income." Right. At my son's urging and against my better judgment, I had put my small nest egg into the hands of a friend of his, a financial "expert," when I should have followed my instincts and put it under my mattress. Now, my only retirement income was likely to be the government's Old Age Security monthly allotments.

Maybe Nordwall Enterprises hadn't been affected. I needed to ask Jason. I dialled his number. My daughter-in-law answered. "Oh, hello Amy, it's Jess. Is Jason there?"

"He's busy at the moment, Jess. Can he call you back?" Amy's tone was distant, as though she were dealing with a demanding client.

"It's important that I talk to him. Is he there?" I could hear the family clatter in the background.

"Nicholas, stop that. I'm talking to Granny." Amy's voice became louder. "He's just going down to his office. He has a *really* important project to deal with. I'll tell him you called."

"I've just heard some bad news and I wanted to talk to him about the investment he suggested. Have you heard of Nordwall Enterprises?" The prolonged silence told me Amy had hung up.

Trust Amy to try and stop me talking to my son without her being in on it. She never passed on my messages, so I dialled Jason's office number.

"Hi, Mum. What's up?"

"Have you heard the news?"

"About the Canucks? Don't tell me you watched a hockey game?"

"No. Not the Canucks. The stock market." Why would I be interested in the bloody Canucks?

"Oh that." Jason sounded bored. "I don't think it's a big deal."

"Well it is for me. Remember Nordwall Enterprises?"

"No. Should I?"

"Well you suggested I go to Robert."

"Oh. Right. I'd forgotten about that. Is Nordwall involved?"

"I don't know. That's what I want you to find out." As he'd been the one to suggest I invest, he should know who to contact.

"Okay, Mum. I'll phone Robert right now and get back to you. Don't worry. I'm sure they'll be fine."

I tried to enjoy my tea, but I found myself pulling my ear lobe, something I've done all my life despite my mother slapping my hand away. Would Jason be able to find out anything? Perhaps Nordwall wasn't affected? I washed up, wiped the counter tops again, and watered the poinsettia that refused to die after its Christmas glory. I couldn't understand why it lived when I tried all means to make it unwelcome, other than dumping it out. I even cursed at it as I'd heard that plants understand when you talk to them. It should have shrivelled from lack of self esteem after I'd finished, but no, it continued to bloom.

What would I do if I'd lost all my savings? I'd never be able to retire, that's all. Not the end of the world when I still had some get up and go left in me. At least I had a house. I found myself humming "Count your blessings one by one." It was a favorite song of my mother's. Gracie Fields used to sing it during the war, evidently, in an effort to cheer up people whose houses had turned into rubble.

My major blessing was the family home that Frank and I built in Kerrisdale after we'd emigrated to Canada. Little did we know, when we saved ten thousand dollars for the lot, that property values in the neighborhood would skyrocket. Those were good days—both of us working, planning and building the house, getting ready to have children. I can never remember when it went sour. But the house turned out to be a great investment. When we sold it, I ended up with enough money to buy a house here in Nelson with something left over to live on into my old age. Or so I'd thought.

The phone rang and I slopped tea down myself. "Not good news, Mum, I'm afraid." Jason sounded like a doctor telling a patient he had inoperable cancer.

"Tell me, Jason." I can't stand waffling.

"Nordwall stocks are down eighty-five percent. But they're still in business. And the good news is…you still have fifteen percent."

"Fifteen percent? That means there's hardly anything left." I wanted to cry. I also wanted to thump Jason for being so cavalier about my money.

"This is going to be a problem for Robert. He's pretty bummed."

"Oh dearie me. Poor Robert."

"They may come up again, Mum. It might be a temporary setback. It's a good company." Jason's voice had a 'there, there,' tone about it.

I didn't answer.

"Mum, are you okay?"

"I'm fine, luv," I managed to say. "I'll do what Brits always do in bad times—have a nice cup of tea."

"Amy and I can help out, you know."

"Thanks, but there's no need. I'll be fine."

"We'll see you tonight and talk about it then."

I had got out of bed in the morning, feeling cheerful, looking forward to the day and then, just a few hours later, I was unemployed, facing poverty, suffering from an injured knee, and had no hot water.

I went out on my small balcony and bellowed at the world, "Bugger you! Bugger you all. You won't get my house, you know. You won't get my house!" With my fists clenched and holding back my tears I began to sing, "There'll be blue birds over, the white cliffs of Dover, tomorrow, just you wait and see."

A small girl making a snowman in her yard across the lane looked up. I waved. She smiled, waved back and carried on digging. I went in to put the kettle on.

2

I SET OFF for dinner with my son. How could he be so—
what's the word?—*nonchalant*, yes nonchalant, with my
money. With my future. He cared more about what happened
to his mate than he did about me. Poor Robert. Bummed was
he? Tough tatties.

I should never have let Jason talk me into investing. I've
always thought it was a risky business, but my mother told
me men know about these things and women don't. And look
at her. When Dad died she didn't even know how to write a
check or how to pay the bills or anything to do with money.
He decided how much she needed for housekeeping, not her,
so we ended up at the end of the week eating bread and chips.

I kicked Jason and Amy's gate open. They lived in a
modern house—well, modern compared with mine—in an
area that had been a quarry. Its garage was a full frontal
assault with the attached house added as an afterthought.
The immaculate bordered path around the garage, the pol-
ished brass mailbox, and the white pedestal vase of artificial

Shasta daisies were a prelude to the hygienic neatness of the interior.

A small boy opened the door and stood holding the handle, smiling.

"Who are you?" I asked looking around. "Have I come to the wrong house?"

"I'm Nicholas," he said with certainty. "And you're Granny."

"No, that's not right. I do have a grandson called Nicholas, but he doesn't look at all like you."

"What does he look like?"

"He's got reddish hair and freckles and brown eyes."

"I've got reddish hair and freckles and brown eyes."

I peered into his face. "Why so you have. But you can't be Nicholas."

"Why not?"

"Because Nicholas is four and you're a baby, not a big boy."

"No I'm not. I'm four." He drew himself up to his full thirty-six inches.

"You might be four, but you're still not Nicholas."

"Why not?"

"Because Nicholas always gives me a big, big hug." He let go of the door and launched himself into my arms and I carried him into the house. Amy was out of sight, thank goodness. She didn't approve of the way I talked to her son. "You are teaching him to lie," she once told me. I ignored her. She's a daft woman when it comes to her kids—or when it comes to anything, for that matter. Whenever I tried to be funny with my grandchildren, she'd bustle about with a stiff look on her face and say things like, "Granny's only joking, you know. Leprechauns aren't scary."

Then there was the time I was telling a story about me fishing for newts and falling in the canal and I used the word *bloody*, which is common enough in Yorkshire and not meant as a swear word. Well, Amy put on a face like a fig and said, "Not in front of the children." I wanted to belt her one. After that I felt like I had to watch every word, which doesn't make for a relaxed visit.

As usual, the place smelled of polish, but also of something delicious cooking. Nicholas led me into the kitchen where Amy stirred ingredients in a wok. "Hi, Jess." She half turned her dark head to lift her face so I could kiss her cheek. A smell of perfume took over from the stirfry. "Dinner's nearly ready."

I turned to the 18-month-old in her high chair. Tapping on her tray I chanted, "Inketty dinketty poppetty pet, the ladies of London they wear scarlet." Julie, the image of her mother, held out a miniature carrot to me in her little dimpled hand and I bit off the end. She giggled and threw the other end on the floor.

"Julie, food is for eating, not throwing." Amy wiped the floor around the high chair with a cloth that smelled of disinfectant.

"Granny, come and see what I've made." Nicholas tugged at my arm.

"Not now, Nicholas. Time to wash your hands," Amy said. "Jess, can you let Jason know that dinner will be on the table in five minutes? He's in his office."

"Nicholas, I'd love to see what you've made. Can you show me after dinner?" I said before I went downstairs.

Jason's office in the basement was reached by a set of wide carpeted stairs. Basement really isn't the right word to describe a level big enough to hold storerooms, a bedroom, bathroom, playroom, and an office, but that's what they called it. Jason was on the phone when I entered. He waved and indicated a chair.

His office, unlike the rest of the house, was not the realm of a tidy person. In fact it was a wonder he knew where anything was. Stacks of file folders spewed their contents over the floor, a bookshelf held cables and computer parts, books were piled on the floor, and you couldn't tell what his desk was made of as there wasn't a bare area to be seen. A large monitor and computer dominated the desk—hardly surprising given his work as a programmer.

The only personal item in the room was a photo of him and two friends laughing over beer steins at some student gathering. Youth and exuberance glowed at me from the frame as I compared his life then with the present. What had happened to the carefree, laid-back, generous son I used to know? Was it simply age or was it being married to Amy? I had never thought she was right for him, but you have to tread very carefully as a mother-in-law.

When Jason finished his conversation he swivelled his chair to face me and spread his hands. "Oh Mum. Look, I'm really sorry about your investment. I wish I hadn't suggested it. But there is hope."

"I'm not holding my breath." I still felt resentful.

"At least you have the house. That's the best investment you ever made."

"Yes," I said. No thanks to you. I stared at him. Was this

the boy I gave birth to and raised? The boy who did a paper route and bought me flowers with his first pay? He used to give me big hugs that lifted me off my feet and we'd go out for a beer and laugh over things like a painted sign that said, "My cow and me welcome thee." I hardly ever saw him on his own any more—Amy made sure of that.

"Let's talk about it after the kids are in bed. Amy will be out, so there'll just be the two of us."

"Dinner's ready," we heard Amy call down the stairs.

Jason stood up and held out his hand to me. "We better hurry. Amy gets upset if we're late."

"Heaven forbid we upset Amy," I said.

"I don't think you understand how fragile she is," Jason said as we hurried upstairs.

Fragile my foot.

We never ate dinner in the kitchen, because Amy liked the formal dining room better. I shifted in my chair and tried to stop pulling my ear.

"Nicholas, sit down," Amy said as she pulled Julie's high chair closer to her. It slid easily on the plastic sheet underneath it.

As Nicholas sat down, he sent his glass of milk flying. Amy said, "Nicholas, I keep telling you to be more careful. Now look what you've done."

I ran into the kitchen for a cloth and mopped up the milk while Amy found a bowl of carpet cleaner and another cloth to scrub the flowered carpet with. If we'd been in the kitchen, with its tile floor, it wouldn't have mattered if the kids spilled stuff. But let's make life difficult for ourselves to keep up appearances.

Nicholas carefully picked out the mushrooms from his stirfry before settling down to eat. I tucked into mine. Whatever I thought about Amy, she was a bloody good cook, and I didn't need to be told about starving children in Africa to enjoy her food.

"Have you heard from Lisa lately?" Amy asked about my daughter in New Zealand.

"Last I heard she was in Rotorua working on the preservation of kiwi birds," I said. "The mail is terrible. I will get two letters close together and then nothing for weeks."

"Julie, eat your broccoli," Amy said as she leaned over to poke at the infant's plate.

"I'll have to get you a computer, Mum, so you can email," Jason said.

Amy laughed. "Jess doesn't need a computer. She can't even use the TV remote you gave her."

Jason stared at Amy briefly, then turned to me.

"Thank you, luv," I quickly said, "but I don't think I've got the gumption to use one."

"Sure you have," Jason said. "I can teach you. It's easy when you know how. And think what you'd save on stamps." He laughed as he always had when he saw me soaking unfranked stamps off of envelopes so I could use them again.

Amy began to collect the plates. "You're busy enough, Jason, without taking on a student."

Jason's mouth set in a firm line, but he didn't say any more.

"Well, Mum," Jason said after the children were in bed and Amy had departed for her Pilates class, "what are you going to do?" He put down a tray of herbal tea in front of the gas fire and turned up its flames. In that light he looked just like his father with his reddish fair hair, soft brown eyes and full lips, which, as a child, could pout dramatically.

"I'm going to look for a job, of course. I'm sure something will show up. An elderly soul needing care, maybe."

"Are you okay for money?" he asked. "We can help out."

"That's good of you, but I can manage."

He leaned forward. "Amy and I think you should come and live with us. We could easily turn the basement into a suite."

"Why? I'm not ga-ga."

"Of course not. But Amy and I want to look after you."

Since his marriage it was always "Amy and I." He wasn't just Jason but a Jason-Amy combo, so I was beginning to think of him as Jamy. My eyes narrowed. "You mean you want a built-in babysitter?"

He paused to pour tea. "There is that," he admitted. "We'd pay you, of course. Then Amy could go back to work and your financial troubles would be over." He leaned back as if he'd solved all my problems.

"I don't need to live in your basement. I have a house." I tried to keep my voice even as I said these words slowly. He didn't pick up the cue.

"Amy and I think you should sell it. Make it work for you. The market is good right now. In fact, Amy has asked a realtor friend to do a market evaluation."

"What?" I could hardly believe him. "How dare she?

You're my son, not my bloody keeper." I got up to find the laundry basket. I needed to do something with my hands. Jason didn't answer. He sat staring at the fire while I began to take small garments out of the basket and thump them into folded shapes.

I thought that he had finally grasped how angry I was until he said, "I know you're upset what with the fire and the investment, but when you're rational again you'll see the sense in it."

My house, built for a tradesman in 1900, had two grander houses on either side. Their gabled roofs looked down on mine, and where they had lawns with trees and shrubs, mine had only a small patch of grass. At the front nothing separated our gardens but a row of high grass where lawn mowers had marked out the property lines. At the back, a garage took up much of my yard and an ivy-covered fence separated me and the vegetable gardens on either side.

I fell in love with the house when I first saw it for sale. Its two dormer windows, capped by small gables, looked like friendly eyes with decorated eyelids, and the curved roof down either side looked like a judge's long wig. A panelled door off a small porch welcomed me when I came home and I loved the smooth feel of the antique brass handle that let me into my haven and the Victorian stained glass window, inset in the front door, which cast a rosy glow into the hall.

The front of the house was level with the road but because it was on a hill, the back, with the basement showing, was higher than the lane that separated my row from the row below. One day, like the neighbors, I wanted to grow vegetables and to plant flowering vines that would camouflage the decrepit garage.

I grew up in a row of smoke-blackened brick houses in Sheffield, England, with a view of a gas works at one end of the street, a belching factory chimney at the other, and washing lines strung across the road. I tried to recall that memory before I looked up my tree-lined street and admired the view of lush green mountains around me. My house represented all I came to Canada for—smoke-free air, natural beauty, freedom from class distinctions, and prosperity. It was mine. I could furnish it how I liked, paint it purple if I wanted to, (I didn't), keep ferrets if I wanted to, (I didn't), or cover the walls with paintings if I wanted to, (I did). It was mine. I bought it by myself, I moved into it by myself and I looked after it by myself. And whatever Amy and Jason said or did, I was keeping it.

3

THE COMPANY OF CRONES held its monthly meetings in a church basement and as they had always been on my day off, I'd been able to go regularly. There were about fifteen of us but only rarely did we all attend. This day there were ten.

There was no age requirement to join, the range being 46 to 92 years, but you had to be a feminist. We supported each other, made each other feel worthy, and above all, we laughed at ourselves. And a good laugh snaps you out of self-pity.

The church basement was gloomy with its concrete floor covered by an indoor-outdoor carpet, its small windows that never lit the room no matter where the sun was, and its low ceiling. Still, it had a kitchen and vases of plastic flowers that were supposed to give the room a cheerful look. And the seats weren't back cripplers.

I didn't really want to go and had dragged myself out of bed with my mother's voice in my head saying, *Feeling sorry for yourself, are you? There's lots of folk far worse off than you.* Yes there were, but that didn't help me cope with no job and no income. Most of the women in Crones struggled with the restrictions of a small income despite having been librarians or teachers or other professionals. Was I going to end up like them?

As usual, Joan was there early to open up and put the coffee on and, as usual, she had made muffins. Always the caregiver, Joan. Even though she was as old as the rest, she fussed around making sure Nina, aged 92, had a seat in a place where she could hear and that Eva, who had only a passing acquaintance with reality, was helped when she was delivered to the door. Yet, when it came to leadership, Joan backed away. There wasn't really a leader anyway; we all chipped in and did what we could. The purpose of the group was to have fun, but what I really enjoyed was that we had all reached a philosophical age when not much upset us. That doesn't mean we were passive—far from it. Most of us had pretty strong views. Nina, for example, was always writing to the *Nelson News* about the latest social injustice, and Claire and Jane were Raging Grannies. What I mean is that we had developed wisdom—or most of us had—which is why we called ourselves 'crones.'

"Hi Jess," Joan said. "I heard about the fire. Are you all right?" She stopped what she was doing to express her concern.

"Yes, thanks," I said. "Unhurt, but unemployed."

"I'll keep my ears open. Lots of volunteer jobs I know of, but not many paid ones. But I'm sure something will turn up." Joan moved to help Eva to her seat.

Laura arrived and immediately launched into an account of her latest visit to her doctor and a description of the wonder drug she'd been prescribed. Everything was wrong with Laura, everything that's expected to go wrong with old people. I didn't hold with it. Just because we age doesn't mean we have to rust. I got really tired of those jokes about constipation and adult diapers, as if that's normal.

Mercifully, Maggie was there. I liked Maggie. She was the youngest, in her forties, but came because she enjoyed talking to older women. She lived just outside Nelson, on her own, and grew her own food, raised chickens, and made herbal remedies. She spent a lot of time outdoors and always looked tanned.

When I first met her I thought she was a Kootenay Woowoo, my term for those who are so busy being "spiritual" they let the world go by, but Maggie wasn't like that. She had a great interest in alternative medicine, if that's the term for healing methods other than Western medicine. Someone told me that she had a degree in botany and worked in the supplement section of the local Co-op.

Maggie was also a joker, even though she appeared to be serious. She was one of those people who can remember jokes and could think of one to suit any occasion. She always told her jokes with a straight face that made them seem even funnier, and she was able to imitate accents to suit.

As we began to settle down, Laura said in a woeful voice, "Now the doctor says I have osteopenia. Can you believe it? As if I don't have enough to put up with." She carefully lowered her bony body onto a chair, delved in her overlarge purse, and pulled out a pill bottle to show us.

"Osteopenia is a diagnosis the pharmaceutical industry has made up. So they can sell you a drug," Maggie said. "It just means your bone mineral density is lower than it was when you were thirty. Perfectly normal."

"Ah, but my doctor has prescribed something to raise it." Laura waved the pill bottle and sat up straight as if to challenge the room to contradict her.

"What are the side effects?" Maggie asked.

"What do you mean?"

"All drugs have side effects," Maggie said. "They're often worse than the condition they're supposed to treat."

"I trust my doctor," Laura said with finality.

"That's your first mistake," I chipped in.

"All you have to do for your bones, what we all have to do, is walk every day and lift a few weights. And now, you can use those exercise machines they've put in the park," Maggie said. "Anyway, do you all realize that Jess has lost her job because of the fire?"

"I use those machines," Nina said. "Some of them, anyway. I can't get on the ones that you're supposed to walk on. I'm frightened of falling off."

Maggie tried again. "You know the restaurant on Baker Street that burned down? Jess lost her job there." She looked round the group.

Eva smiled and nodded. She did that when she didn't know what was going on. That day she had all her buttons done up the right way and her hair combed. I looked to see if she had shoes on because she often showed up in slippers that had Right and Left written on them in black marker.

Fran launched into a story about her fight with the Health Authority. "When my sister went into that rehab center, she could walk with a walker. Now she can't walk at all, after only six weeks. I've been trying to get her moved to St. Margaret's, but they say she can't change."

Eva nodded and smiled at Fran. "I'm Catholic too."

Laura held out her thin wrists to Maggie. "Look at those. Don't you think I'm headed for osteoporosis?"

Maggie ignored her.

"No, you're headed for death by medicine," I muttered, and then I told everyone about the Grizzly fire. "So that's put paid to my job."

"You can always sell your house," Joan said.

"That's true. But then where do I live? How long do you think that money would last?" If I sounded irritated, I was. Selling my only asset was a quick fix but not a long-term solution.

"Jess needs a job," Maggie, bless her, said. "So if anyone hears of anything, could they let Jess know?"

"Thanks, Maggie," I said, "and while I'm not working I could come to the Stitch and Bitch sessions. Are they still Thursday afternoons?"

In addition to their monthly meeting, the Crones had a sewing circle that met every week and a book club that met once a month. I liked to cross-stitch, and it's much more fun to do it with others.

"Yes," Laura said. "Next week it's at my place. It will be good to have you join us."

At that point, our guest speaker arrived to talk about living wills. She was a community health nurse who specialized in geriatrics and after she'd introduced herself, she struck me as being sensible enough to listen to. She had us all tell her who we were and what was our biggest worry about dying. We had talked about this many times; most of us were afraid of not being allowed to die in peace, or of being in pain. Eva got away with it by saying with a beatific smile, "Jesus loves us."

The nurse gave us each a package that included a thirteen-page form we were to fill out, copy, and give to people who would likely oversee our care during our last days. We went over the form. The biggest discussion arose over the "What I Want: Considering life support and medical interventions" section. Laura, of course, chose the "I still want to have all necessary medical interventions."

"What for, when you're dying?" I asked her.

"They might be able to do something. You never know."

"What? Give you another forty-eight hours of struggle?" I may have sounded as if I were talking to a nitwit because I was. "The trouble today is that no one's allowed to die in peace. Everyone tries to keep you breathing when you're trying to leave, and they thump your heart when it's trying to stop."

Maggie lightened the atmosphere. "There was this man in a pub who said, 'Last night, my wife and I were sitting in the living room and I said to her, 'I never want to live in a vegetative state, dependent on some machine and fluids from a bottle. If that ever happens, just pull the plug.' She got up, unplugged the TV and then threw out my beer. Bitch...'"

We all laughed, especially the nurse.

"There should be a law or at least a moral code," Maggie said. "Thou shalt not strive officiously to keep people alive."

"But lots of people have survived heart attacks," Laura said, "and gone on to live an active life. How do you know if you're not like that when the time comes?"

"If you've been lying dying in a hospital for weeks, you're not likely to rise again," I said. "I think it's inhumane to try and revive someone like that. Put a plastic bag over my head and have done with it. That's what I want."

"It's important to let your wishes be known, even if we can't meet them," the nurse said looking at me. "Filling in these forms now, while you are of sound mind, is important. Everyone has different views as you can see. Health professionals do try to respect your wishes—but plastic bags are not in our procedure manual. Now, are there any questions?"

Fran asked about Power of Attorney. The nurse explained that this enabled you to appoint someone to deal with financial affairs, but did not apply to health care decisions.

I bet Amy would like power over me so they can sell my house and run my life; all for my own good, of course.

"Any more questions?" the nurse asked.

"What shouldn't you covet?" Eva said, nodding.

"Sorry. Say that again." The nurse looked puzzled.

"Thou shalt not covet," Eva said. "But what?"

The nurse walked over and took hold of Eva's hands. "It's thy neighbor's ass, isn't it?"

Eva looked up at her and smiled. "Yes, that's right. I've never wanted an ass."

"Neither have I," the nurse said as she went back to her seat.

I can't say I felt any better by the end of our meeting, but just as I was leaving Maggie put her arms around me and asked if I'd like some frozen rhubarb from her last year's garden. I'm very fond of rhubarb and custard so I enthusiastically said, "Yes please."

We moved out of the church into the spring sunshine. "You must be feeling at a loose end now you're not working. Would you like to come over to my place for lunch?"

We set a day and I went home feeling I could cope with life after all, even though that life meant more job hunting. There are two things I hate above all else: trying on bathing suits and job hunting.

4

I STARTED MY SEARCH for a job by going to the library and studying the ads in the local papers. I didn't expect to find anything as I knew that many arrangements in Nelson, such as apartment rentals and help wanted, are the result of word of mouth. My best bet was to talk to people I know and to inquire in cafés and restaurants. I searched *Pennywise* and was delighted to find someone looking for a part-time care aide for a young disabled man. Just up my alley. I phoned the number. No, they wanted a male.

I sauntered along Baker Street and called in at the numerous cafés and restaurants but they were all very sorry, they didn't need anyone. Then I bumped into Felix, the owner of the Grizzly Grill. He told me that Bob's Café needed help and that Bob was interviewing applicants that evening, after the café closed. Feeling more hopeful, I went home and phoned Bob for an appointment.

Dressed in my smart pants and shirt, I headed down the hill about 8:30, slowly because my knee was still a bit sore. It seemed funny to be walking down the familiar route in the dark. Normally I went to work mid-morning.

Bob's was on one of the side streets off Baker and was popular with people who liked a hearty meal at a low price. Stodge, I called it.

The lone occupant of the café was a young woman with dyed blonde hair, heavy makeup, a nose stud, and a leather jacket. Her perfume mingled with the stale cooking smells that hung about the place, and she sat at a plastic-covered table reading a magazine.

"It's closed," she said when I walked in.

"I know," I said. "I've come for a job interview."

The youngster looked me up and down before saying, with emphasis, "*You?*" She rolled her eyes. "Are you serious?"

"Why not me?"

"Whatever." She shrugged and got up to take off her leather jacket and hang it over a chair.

I picked up a magazine and sat across the room from Miss Clever Clogs. I could feel her staring at me as I pretended to be engrossed in an article about broad beans. Suddenly she was beside me. "People your age shouldn't be taking jobs," she hissed.

"And who would pay my rent?" I said quelling my instinct to belt her one.

Fortunately a harassed-looking man in a white apron came in. "Which one of you is Jess?" I stood up. "I'm Bob. Come into the back."

Bob led me into a cubicle off the kitchen where he did his paper work. He pulled up a stool for me and sat on the swivel desk chair. "Felix recommended you," he said. "Are you still up to waiting on tables?"

"Of course," I said. "I was working at the Grill last week." What a daft question. I hadn't grown decrepit in the last few days. I examined Bob as a prospective employer. He looked ordinary enough: mid-forties, small mustache, short hair, overweight; not the sort to pinch bottoms or peer down blouses, even though the calendar behind his head displayed a naked woman looking over one shoulder and bending down with her bum stuck out.

Bob explained the hours, the pay, days off, and his expectations. "I have other applicants. Why should I pick you?"

"I'm reliable. I show up on time. My customers like me because I actually *wait* on them and make sure they have everything they need without being intrusive." I'd rehearsed this speech in anticipation of the question.

Bob grunted. "Right, I'll let you know tomorrow. What's your phone number?" He made his only notes on me in a spiral daybook. "Send the other one in."

I told Miss Clever Clogs to go in and left.

The following morning Bob phoned to tell me he'd given the job to the other applicant.

"Why?" I asked.

There was a slight pause. "Well," he said slowly, "I know you're experienced, but this job means hard work. You're on your feet all day."

"I know that," I said. "I've been doing it for years."

"Yes, you do have experience."

"You think I'm too old?"

"I didn't say that."

"You didn't have to."

After my car had lurched down Maggie's dirt drive I expected to see a log house or a rough cabin, so I was surprised when it turned out to be a large heritage building, with a greenhouse attached. I parked outside an open shed housing a tractor, a small blue car, a wheelbarrow and several bikes.

I got out and looked around at the property with its raised beds, newly planted in neat rows. A large, black, slathery dog barked at me and then, after deciding I was a friend, came wagging to have a sniff.

Maggie appeared at the head of some steep wooden steps and called out a greeting. I had looked forward to this lunch. Maggie would listen to my job searching stories and might have some good ideas about what else I could do. She was a wonderful listener. Didn't chip in with her own stuff, but let you talk and encouraged you with questions.

"Good to see you, Jess." Maggie gave me a big hug and led me into a sunny kitchen. Now there was a room that belonged in a farmhouse—an Aga stove, large saucepans hanging from hooks, shelves of bottled fruit and vegetables, a freshly baked loaf on a rack, and a lovely smell of baking.

"Wow," I said. "Do you grow all your own food?"

"Mostly. I buy grains and fish, but I grow veggies and fruit. And I keep a few hens for eggs and chicken. Other meat I get from farmers I know."

"Did you grow up on a farm?"

"No. I was raised here. This was our family home, but I wouldn't call it a farm. We've always had fruit trees and a garden."

Maggie moved over to the stove and stirred the contents of a large pot. "I hope you don't mind having your main meal at lunch time—because I'm serving venison stew."

"Sounds wonderful." I didn't tell her that I was down to one meal a day supplemented by tea and toast.

"A neighbor gave me some venison, so we're having stew and dumplings. Come and sit here." Maggie pointed to a round wooden table in a window alcove and I sat and looked at her view of trees, a river, and distant snow-topped mountains. How peaceful. Just like Maggie.

"Do you live alone?" I asked.

"Yes, since my mother passed away. That's nearly five years ago now." Maggie stirred something in a pot. "You knew her of course. I used to bring her to Crones. Which is why I still go, even though I'm younger."

"I didn't know her very well. She was poorly a lot, I remember." I recalled a haggard woman with a walker, almost crippled with arthritis, who showed up at Crones occasionally.

"Yes, I was always taking her to the doctor." Maggie chuckled. "Which is why I avoid Western medicine now."

I got up to look down on the property. "The garden must be a lot of work."

"I haven't got anything else to do. It's worth it."

"I thought you worked at the Co-op."

"Part-time. Two days a week." Maggie ladled a delicious-looking brown stew into bowls. "I'm in the vitamins and health products section."

"So that's how you know about drugs?"

"My degree is in botany. I studied how Indigenous people use plants as medicines. And I took a course in homeopathy."

Maggie put a bowl of stew in front of me, then reached for the loaf, which she cut into chunks. A green salad completed the meal.

I didn't need an invitation to begin eating. I ate as if I hadn't seen a decent meal for ages. Which I hadn't. I bet Maggie had put on this substantial meal because she understood that I was desperate.

After I'd finished my second bowl of stew, Maggie asked, "How's the job search?"

"I've applied for a couple of waitressing jobs and been turned down. I've been to most of the retail shops on Baker but no luck." I had a thought. "Anything at the Co-op, do you think?"

"There's a waiting list. I only got in there because I know about supplements. Have you tried Crawfords?"

"No. I hadn't thought of that." Crawfords was a small factory just outside of town.

Maggie looked thoughtful. "You could make your house work for you. Rent out some space, take in students…"

"I'd hate that. My house is my refuge. But maybe I'll have to." I took a sip of the herbal tea Maggie had made. "I thought of driving a truck, but I think you have to take a course."

Maggie laughed. "I can't see you driving a ten-ton truck!"

"I wouldn't be able to reach the pedals. Or climb into the bloody thing. I also thought of holding signs at road works. But my best bet is some sort of care aide."

"Have you put an ad in the *Pennywise* under Work Wanted?"

"No. I'll do that. And I'll go to Crawfords."

I left Maggie's with the remains of the loaf, a bag of vegetables, a dozen eggs, and an infusion of hope.

The next day I visited the highways department in City Hall. I wanted to find out how to apply for a job holding signs at road works. The people who do that often looked quite old, and they were on their feet all day, something I was used to. Would I be up to standing out in the wet and cold, inhaling car fumes and running the risk of being knocked down?

The helpful clerk told me the department doesn't directly hire but contracts the job out to other companies. She gave me a phone number to call.

"Triple SA. Nancy speaking. How may I help you?"

"Hi. My name's Jess and I'm looking for information about working in traffic control." I tried to make my voice matter-of-fact rather than pleading.

"What did you want to know, Jess?"

I hesitated. The voice seemed kind so I said, "I'm looking for work and I wondered if I'd be any good at holding up Stop and Slow signs."

"You need a good personality—one that is public relations-oriented, because you're usually dealing with frustrated drivers. And you have to be able to stand for a long time."

"I think I can do that," I said with feeling. "I've been a waitress."

"Then you're used to the public. That's good. You need a car, of course. We supply a vest and a hard hat, but you need your own boots."

I ran an ancient Honda Civic that managed to splutter along, but the only boots I possessed were at least thirty years old and looked it.

"You have to take a course before you can apply," Nancy continued. "A traffic control course. It's for two days at Selkirk College. Two hundred dollars."

Oh bugger, I thought, where am I going to get that? "Right," I said, "how much does the job pay?"

"Twelve dollars an hour. And workdays are six to eighteen hours long."

"Have you ever done it?"

"I've done it for years." Nancy sounded enthusiastic. "Love it. I like being outside. You never get bored. But the best thing is, there's no boss. No one standing over you. I like that."

"Are there jobs available?"

"Not right now. But they come up quite often. You have to have the course to apply."

Nancy didn't seem anxious to ring off so I said, "Do you mind if I ask you why you're in the office now? Is it an age thing?"

"No, there's no age limit, I'm sixty-four. I had to have surgery on my knee so they put me in here for a while. But I'd rather be outside." She paused. "Good luck."

This job sounded promising, but where was I to get two hundred dollars? Not only that, good work boots cost a bomb. Jason had offered to help, but I didn't want to borrow from him. I had just received my last paycheck from Felix, which included holiday pay. The bill for the water tank came at the same time. That bill took care of most of my pay or I could have afforded the course.

I reviewed my expenditures. The house was the most costly. I had turned down the thermostat to 64 degrees, which wasn't bad while the weather was getting warmer, and I turned down the new hot water tank to its lowest setting, making the water barely warm. But the economy that really upset me was canceling my foster child in India. I'd supported her for six years and watched her grow from a toddler into a smiling schoolgirl. I pulled out the latest picture of her, standing proud in her school uniform beside her sari-ed mother. "I'm sorry, Sonali, I'm so sorry," I whispered.

I searched the Help Wanted columns every day. If I'd been a fork-lift operator, a tennis instructor, a hairdresser, a jewelry maker, or a whiz at Excel, I'd have been in luck. As it was, there was nothing for a useless old lass like me. I did apply as a caregiver to a handicapped toddler, but they wanted a registered nurse. In the end I stopped looking at ads and took to wandering up and down Baker Street saying hello to people I know and staring into shop windows.

5

AMY PHONED one day and asked me out for lunch. She had never done that before, but then I was working and couldn't have gone anyway. Sometimes she and friends would show up at the Grizzly Grill for lunch. I tried to hand them over to another server but it didn't always work, and I was forced to wait on them. Why did she come to the Grizzly, anyway? The food was not the sort she liked. Was it to make me feel inferior. I half expected her to snap her fingers at me and shout, "Waitress!"

I had no excuse to refuse her offer of lunch, and besides, I needed a good meal.

"Where would you like to go?" she said.

"Not Bob's Café," I said.

"No way. The food there's terrible. How about Max and Irma's?"

I rarely ate out so I was pleased and psyched myself up to be pleasant. I wanted a harmonious family relationship above all else, and hers was the only family I was going to get. Lisa seemed to have settled in New Zealand and anyway, her love interests were always women, so grandchildren were unlikely.

The real problem, I had to admit, was that I didn't like Amy—never had. What Jason sees in her is beyond me. He'd always been a laid-back, happy-go-lucky sort of lad, generous with money and generous in spirit. Whereas Amy was the opposite. I'd dropped some coins in a homeless man's hat as we walked along Baker Street one day and she'd said, "I don't know why you do that, Jess. It only encourages them."

"Everyone falls on hard times once in a while, and jobs aren't that easy to find." For a social worker, Amy showed little compassion or understanding.

She took on a righteous expression and said, "It's just a matter of perseverance. Besides, everyone should save for a rainy day." I wanted to sock her one right in that prissy face.

"You never know what a person's story is," I said. "There are lots of reasons for hardship."

"Tell me about it! I hear sob stories all the time. Most people should just smarten up."

Amy used the word *should* so often that I assumed she came from a religious background. But that was not the case. She was tight-lipped about her past, but from the occasional random remark I gathered she had grown up near Salmon Arm in a family where no one seemed to have a regular job and going to school was an unavoidable trial to be endured for as short a time as possible. Evidently she had had no contact with her family since she'd left home. I had never met her parents, who hadn't been at their wedding, and Jason and the children never referred to their grandparents.

Amy had broken away and put herself through college. I admired her for that, but there was something about her I couldn't quite put my finger on. Was it fear? Fear of doing the wrong thing, of disobeying society's rules, of not appearing "normal"? Fear of poverty? By marrying Jason she was assured of a steady income and a middle-class lifestyle. Perhaps she was afraid of losing that.

"How's the job hunting?" she asked after we'd sat down and ordered.

"No luck so far. They think I'm too old."

Amy said nothing and I had the impression she agreed with them. I stared at the chalkboards showing the specials before finally breaking the silence with, "How's Nicholas enjoying gymnastics?"

"He loves it! He needs to move his body. Like most boys."

"Now that I'm not working I'd like to spend more time with him. Perhaps he could come over to play at my house? Or I could take him to the park?" I offered.

Amy took a sip of water. "He's already pretty busy. I believe that children should be kept occupied."

"You don't think spending time with his grandmother is important, then?" I stared at her.

"Yes, of course. Which is why we like to have you for dinner every week."

I wanted to be a Granny to my grandchildren, not just someone who came to Sunday dinners. I wanted to take them to the beach, have fun, buy them treats they weren't allowed at home—that sort of thing. But Amy had other ideas. She always had to be in charge, always the supervisor ready to correct.

On one rare occasion when I had taken the children on

the tram and bought them an ice cream in the park, Amy had greeted them with, "Look at you both! You've got ice cream all down your shirts." Then she turned to me and said, "They're not allowed ice cream. It's full of sugar."

The food arrived and I tucked in while Amy carefully cut a piece of her lasagne before switching the fork to her right hand—the American way. What a stupid way of eating—as if you've never grown past having your food cut up for you as a kid.

I began to feel the strain of having to make conversation. Was it going to be one of those times when I asked questions and Amy answered them? I decided to say nothing and leave it to her. I wasn't going to let her spoil my food.

Finally Amy said, "Jason wanted me to take you out now you're unemployed."

"Thank you," was all I said.

"What sort of job would you like?" Amy had her listening face on. "Being on your feet all day is hard."

"I'm used to it."

"Have you tried for other waitress jobs?" Amy was using her official social worker voice, as if she was interviewing a client.

"Of course." I wasn't going to be chatty if it killed me.

She continued to eat, oh so delicately, while I finished my meat pie and chips, scraped the plate noisily and clanked my knife and fork together.

We sat in silence. I looked around the room. The place used to be a funeral home and the pizza oven was where they cremated bodies. Or so rumor had it. A thirty-year old woman at the next table gazed admiringly into her date's eyes as if his every word was a gem. Lassie, are you that desperate? I looked everywhere but at Amy.

She paid attention to the menu on the wall as if she hadn't seen it before and then asked me if I liked artichokes.

"Not Jerusalem ones," I said. "They give me wind."

That ended that conversation.

We got up to go and Amy paid the bill, I noticed that she gave about five percent as a tip. Typical. I surreptitiously took a five-dollar bill out of my purse and put it on the table before I followed Amy out.

She suggested a browse on Baker Street. We sauntered along for a while and then she stopped. "Oh look at those Jimmy Choo's. The red ones."

"Two hundred and fifty dollars for a pair of shoes!" I could hardly believe it. They were completely impractical with idiotic high heels and silly little straps.

"That's not bad. You should see the prices in Vancouver." Amy moved on down the street.

"Think how many people could be fed for two-hundred-and-fifty-dollar donation to the food bank."

She stopped to look at me. "Food bank! Food banks encourage laziness. Besides, the government should take care of that sort of service."

I stopped walking and glared at her. "Well they don't, so what are people supposed to do? Lie down and die?"

Amy's face had that wooden expression of self-righteous smugness. "There's always work if you look hard enough."

I so badly wanted to give her a kick up the ass that I had to leave. "Thank you for lunch. I have to go now," I managed to say, and marched away.

6

MY SILVER SPOON with *Whitby* written on the handle scraped the tea caddy as I scooped the last of my tea leaves into the pot. *Beyond the Fringe* had a skit where, in the wake of fresh wartime disasters Will said to his wife, "Never mind, dear. Put the kettle on and we'll have a nice cup of tea." As things got worse the final line was, "Never mind, dear. Put the kettle on and we'll have a nice cup of hot water." Was I reduced to a nice cup of hot water?

I scrounged around the house looking for things I could sell. Storage boxes in the basement yielded an electric typewriter I had once used for a typing course, a baseball glove belonging to Jason, a couple of cast iron frying pans, a July 1969 newspaper showing pictures of the lunar landing, piles of Lisa's "art" work from pre-school, a painted wooden clog my mother brought back from Holland, and a carefully wrapped Royal Doulton tea set that was far too fragile for everyday use, but might fetch a buck or two. I took it upstairs ready to take it to—where? I'd never been in a pawn shop, and besides, I didn't want it back. An ad in *Pennywise*, that was it.

Upstairs my furniture looked anything but saleable. Who would want the bedroom set Frank and I bought for two hundred dollars when we first arrived in Vancouver? Or the stool Jason made in high school? All my furniture was utilitarian. Where had I bought it? When? And what would I use if I did sell it?

The only thing of value I owned was my cameo brooch. I cradled it in my hand as I stroked the head of Ceres. My grandmother, a down-to-earth Lancashire woman who worked in a mill all her life, and managed to raise six children as well, gave it to me. The brooch had been left to her by an equally penniless aunt, and she would never have thought of selling it even in the direst financial straits. Her only granddaughter would not sell it either.

I was now down to the last of things: the last loaf of bread, the last pat of butter, the last spud, the last dollar. The shelf that used to hold cans and boxes now simply showed dust outlines of where these items had lain. I had been broke many times since I left Frank, but there had always been a paycheck on the horizon. In one of those temporary periods, I had lived on bread and eggs for two weeks and learned how a few herbs can liven up an omelette.

The idea that I should visit the food bank hovered beside me like a Halloween ghoul, a nasty piece of work that jeered at me in my mother's voice: *Useless old woman, you're a waste of space; now you have to beg for food; taker, taker, taker; always proud of yourself that you gave to charities. Now look at you—a scrounger.*

Outside the church basement that housed the Nelson Food Cupboard sat a giant bell, cast in 1895 and rung in the church through its various denomination changes. I hovered beside it as if interested in examining the plaque until the street was empty of people. Then I quickly slipped between the double doors into a dark hall. *So you're going to do it are you,* my mother's voice said contemptuously. *Think the world owes you a living, do you?*

An open door on my right led into a large meeting room. I took a big breath and stepped in.

A bulky, bearded man in a navy peaked cap, who could have been a sea captain, greeted me. "Hello," he said in a friendly tone, "what's your name?" He sat behind a table with some sort of a register in front of him.

"Jess," I said in a low voice.

"Speak up, m'dear. Did you say, Bess?"

"No. Jess. Jess Kemp. I haven't been here before and I'm sorry I need you and I will pay you back as soon as I have a job and some money and I have contributed a lot in the past and I never thought I'd need to do this but…"

I paused for breath and he took the opportunity to break in. "Jess, you don't need to explain. We don't ask questions. We only need a name and gender and how many you are feeding for our records. We assume you need food and we're here to provide it. Now this is what you do." He stood up and came round the table. "Sit there until Jean calls you in." He indicated a row of chairs behind me. "Then she'll take you to the storage room where you take what you need. You've brought bags. Good." He smiled down at me. "No need to worry. You've helped others before—now it's your turn.

Everyone goes through tough times." He patted my arm and returned to his table.

I turned round to the chairs and Claire, one of the Crones, sat there smiling at me. What on earth was she doing here? "Hi Jess." She tapped on the chair beside her. "You're fourth in line. It's not busy today. How are you? How's the job hunting?"

She was so matter-of-fact, so nonchalant, as if it was perfectly natural to meet in a food bank. Now she knew I needed a food bank, I bet she would tell the other Crones. Then everyone would know. How would I be able to look them all in the face again? I could almost hear them whispering: "There's Jess. Used to be a waitress here in town. Now she goes to the food bank, if you can believe it."

To answer her question, I said, "Not so good. No one wants older women."

"Yeah, we've had our uses. Now we're dispensable," Claire said. She's the leading light in the Raging Grannies. Sometimes her extreme feminism gets up my nose, especially when she blames everything on the patriarchy. "But what do you expect," she went on, "in a patriarchal society?"

I wished it were her turn to go in and collect her food so I could get out of there. I fiddled with my shopping bags. "Do you come here often?" I finally asked her.

"Couple of times a week. Be sure to come on Wednesdays. They have fresh meat."

"Really? I thought food banks only supplied non-perishables."

"No, we get fresh veggies and sometimes there's meat other days, but Wednesdays for sure." Claire heaved her substantial frame to its feet. "It's my turn. See ya."

I sniffed the smell of unwashed bodies and dirty clothes that I'd encountered before when dealing with the homeless. He was an unshaven man of indeterminate age dressed in layers of clothing, mostly ex-army, and a Peruvian woolen hat that gave his head a strange shape, like a beetle. He carried his possessions in a bundle. I bet he'd left a shopping cart outside the church. His eyes darted from side to side, but he took no notice of me. "Hello," I said, and for a moment his bright blue eyes met mine before they resumed their anxious, jerky glances.

Was closing mental hospitals a bright idea? It wouldn't have been so disastrous if some other form of care had been put in their place, but it hadn't, and now people who cannot take care of themselves were left helpless and discarded. My fists clenched. How can this wealthy society leave people like this to fend for themselves? I was glad when the door opposite opened and an efficient woman in a navy apron beckoned me in to a shelf-lined room with two large refrigerators. Cans of beans and vegetables were neatly stacked on the shelves that also held boxes of tea, cereal and sugar, jars of jam, peanut butter, rice, and stacks of fresh vegetables. To my delight there was a jar of Robertson's marmalade, a treat I rarely allowed myself.

"I'm Jean," she said. "Now you haven't been here before, have you?" I shook my head. "So if you're low on staples you may need quite a lot this time. Go around and help yourself. Look in the fridges too."

Jean showed me how the supplies were organized into sections, such as canned vegetables, cereals, etc. "Take one item from each section," she said, "but more if you need it."

My stack of groceries grew. I took a can of peas and quickly put it back. I had too much. More than my fair share. I tried to ignore the ghoul chanting in my ear: *greedy guts, useless, can't pull your weight, social pariah.*

Jean came to help me pack my loot into my bags. "You haven't got much. Here, take another couple of cans of beans and some more flour. You can't bake with that." She replaced my small bag of flour with a larger bag. "The bread's on a table on your way out."

"Where does all this come from?" I asked.

"Organizations like SHARE and local stores like Kootenai Moon provide some of it," she said glancing at cases of canned goods waiting to be unpacked, "but we would rather have money donated so we can shop ourselves and get what we know we need. Then we can provide more fresh food. We get a discount, so we can get more for our dollars than an individual can."

"Well I'm extremely grateful." I hoisted my two bulging bags ready to leave by a door other than the one I had come in.

I worked my way around an old shopping cart in the hall and left the church. A wind rustled the trees and on it Swan seemed to float down the hill toward me. Her hair had grown since I last saw her, the day of the fire, and she had removed the long purple strand. She might have looked normal, but she was draped in multi-colored scarves of varying lengths and textures so that she resembled a tropical insect borne on the wind.

"Hey, Jess, howzit going?" She sounded pleased to see me, and I would have greeted her warmly too if she hadn't seen me come out of the food bank. Whatever would she think? That I couldn't handle life?

I set down my bags. "Everything's gone to pot," I said.

Swan's eyes widened and she gave me a delighted grin. "Really? Awesome." She picked up my bags. "Here, I'll carry these home for you." There was something endearing about her don't-give-a-shit attitude; if only some of it would rub off on me.

As we set off she said, "Great idea. I didn't think you had it in you."

I stopped. "Had what in me?"

"I thought you said you were growing pot?" Swan put down the bags and rubbed her hands.

"Of course I'm not growing pot." I began to walk again.

"Lots of people do." Swan gestured to the houses around us before picking up the bags again. "They say that one in four houses in Nelson have grow-ops. And you own your own house. That's huge."

I grimaced at her. "I wouldn't know how."

Swan was swinging the bags beside me. "We can fix that easy enough."

"Don't be silly."

"Haven't you just been to the food bank?"

I could hardly deny the fact. "Yes. I can't get a job. Too old. So I've no money."

"Does your house have a basement?"

I nodded.

"Then make it work for you." A gust of wind blew Swan's scarves around her so she looked like one of those wind-sock decorations outside the toy shop.

I slowed my pace.

"How's your knee?" Swan asked.

"Still a bit sore." How could I get back to the topic of pot without sounding too interested. "Do you grow? Pot, I mean."

"Nah. I live in an apartment. But I help out people who do. Water when they're away. Trim. Pays well."

We were nearly at my house. "Would you like to come in for tea?"

"Some other time. I have to be at work soon."

"Oh, did you get a job? Good for you. Where?"

"The deli on Kootenay. Part-time. I'm still looking around."

I opened the door and Swan brought in the groceries. How could I get her to stay so I could find out more about pot growing? "I'd love to hear about your job. Are you sure you can't stay?"

"Oh, okay."

I put the kettle on. Swan lifted the bags of groceries on to the counter and began to empty them.

"Hungry?" I asked. Swan nodded.

"I can offer you a peanut butter and jelly sandwich, courtesy of the food bank." I took the loaf and two jars from the counter and prepared to make sandwiches. I couldn't open the jars, as usual, and handed them to Swan to unscrew.

As I spread the bread, Swan fiddled with the SPCA calendar on the wall. "As soon as I have a house, I'm going to get a dog like that," she said, pointing to a picture of a black Labrador. "Why don't you have a dog? Don't you like them?"

"I love dogs. But I've been working too much to look

after one properly. I might get one now." Except I couldn't afford to feed myself, let alone a dog.

I made tea and we sat at my small kitchen table facing the window and the view of Elephant Mountain. There was still snow on it, which, in Nelson, meant don't plant your vegetable garden yet. Swan sat cross-legged on her chair. If I sat like that I'd seize up and never be able to stand again.

"So you're suggesting I grow pot for a living?" I said as I poured tea.

Swan laughed. "Why not?"

"It's illegal. I might end up in jail."

She stared at me through her heavily made-up lashes. "Have you looked in the mirror lately? You look like everyone's favorite grandma with that white hair. It's the perfect cover."

I chewed a few times. Peanut butter and jam on white bread is not what I normally eat. A glob stuck to the roof of my mouth and I poked a finger in to dislodge it. "You mean my age is actually in my favor?"

Swan laughed. "Seriously, Marcus could set you up." She jumped up to tear a piece off the newspaper, scribbled on it and laid it on the table. "Here's his phone number."

"Don't be daft, Swan. Of course I can't start a grow-op," I said, but my insides vibrated. Why shouldn't I? Or at least find out more about it.

"If you decide you want to know more, give him a call. Here's my number too." Swan wrote a number on the same scrap of paper.

"Right," I said pulling on my ear lobe. "Trouble is, I don't have any money."

"His deal is that he pays for everything, takes half of what you make for three grows, then you pay him back for the supplies. Easy peasy."

I stared at her. "How much do you make? I always think it's millions."

"Nah. You'll have room for four lights probably. Maybe three. If you're lucky you might get a pound per light. Might. Right now it sells for two thousand a pound. So you'd get eight thousand for a crop about every three months. Maybe."

Eight thousand dollars every three months. Thirty-two thousand a year. That's more than waitressing full time.

"I wouldn't want to get into selling," I said hastily. If I went to Baker Street who would I deal with? How would I even begin?

"You wouldn't have to. Marcus does that." Swan finished her sandwich and stood up. "I'll help you too. Think about it. Gotta fly. Thanks for lunch." She fluttered out.

I sat with a second cup of tea and stared out the window. The idea was preposterous. Of course it was. Then I got to thinking about my financial situation.

My meagre unemployment insurance barely covered house costs and wouldn't last long. Eventually I would get the government's old age payments, maybe a thousand a month. After house and car expenses, that would leave me about a hundred a week for food, clothes, household items, and entertainment. No holidays; no dinners out; no new clothes.

Eight thousand dollars every three months. Tax free too. Just for growing a few plants in the basement. What if I got caught? Would I go to jail? What if I lost the house, then where would I be? I would be a criminal. Bugger that when there's those big wigs running corporations making their millions and not paying taxes. Why should I care? I'd tried to get a job but no one wanted an old prune like me. What was it Swan said? I look too much like everyone's grandma with my snowy hair—but that would work in my favor as no one would ever imagine I would have a grow-op. Not someone my age. Because we're all past it. Well bugger that for a lark.

I could go and live with Jason and Amy, I supposed. They said they would build me a suite. But it would still be in Amy's neat and tidy house. I looked round at my comfortable old chair with its worn cover, the newspaper strewn around, dead leaves from the poinsettia on the floor, an apple waiting to go mouldy enough to throw away, snapshots poked into picture frames, and I knew my lifestyle would be unacceptable. I imagined Amy's disapproving face as she walked in, and she would walk in; it would be *her* house, not *my* home.

In their house there were no displays of snapshots—of the kids at the beach or of a laughing family. Instead there were framed formal studio portraits. There's one of Amy sitting bolt upright with the children on either side of her and Jason standing behind her with his hands on her shoulders. They only needed to be dressed in black and they would make the perfect Victorian family.

I loved the children, but I didn't want them on a daily basis—and I certainly didn't want to be responsible for them. Amy would have too many rules that I would be sure to break. And she wouldn't like the way I said things like "daft bugger." There was, in her mind, a correct way to express yourself. For example, she couldn't say *died*; she had to say *passed*. Passed? Passed what? Water? Gas? No, I'd go crazy in their house.

I've always worked hard, usually at jobs that don't pay well. Women's jobs; service jobs like nurse's aide, child-minding, waiting on tables; jobs that if men did them would pay twice as much. I laughed. The righteous do not inherit the earth, that's for sure.

I picked up the piece of paper with Marcus's number and carefully pinned it to my message board.

7

SUNDAY DINNER with Jason's family had been a ritual since they moved to Nelson. Helping with the children's bath and reading bedtime stories followed the meal, and after that the adults had a chance to talk. I had missed two Sundays with made-up excuses: an impending cold the first time and volunteering at the Capitol theater the second. Now I had to confront my resistance. Jason had made it quite clear that their agenda for me was to live with them as a built-in baby-sitter. It was the last thing on my wish list, but I didn't feel like fighting over it.

To get ready for dinner with them I made oatmeal cookies with my food bank supplies and arrived at their house vowing to keep calm. If the topic of my moving in came up, I would be casual but firm. I would not get my knickers in a twist.

Nicholas commandeered me the moment I arrived to show me a castle he had built with his blocks. "Wow," I said. "That's *awe-some*," a word I had learned from Swan. "Where do you go in?"

He was pointing out the features of his creation when Julie toddled in and sent the whole thing crashing. Nicholas gave her a furious push and she fell on her bum, howling. I was about to pick her up when Amy flew in and glared at me before cuddling Julie. "What's going on?" she demanded.

"Julie knocked over my castle," Nicholas said.

"And what did you do?"

"Nothing."

Now I would have left it there, but Amy needed to use this as a 'teaching moment.' Still cuddling Julie she said, "Nicholas, you're the big boy. Julie is just a baby. Babies are not for hitting."

"She knocked over my castle."

"You are still not to hit her."

"I didn't."

Amy turned to me. "Granny, did Nicholas hit Julie?"

I ignored her and got down on the floor and started to rebuild the castle. I was not going to be made judge and jury. "Nicholas, does this block go here? Show me; I don't know how to build castles."

Dinner passed without incident, but I was on guard the whole time, waiting for some comment about my living arrangements. I had to admit that Amy was a good cook and her table was immaculate. I tried not to eat as if this were my last supper, but I did have twice my normal helping and I could have eaten more, but I didn't want them to suspect that my diet was wanting. "I was so busy I missed lunch today," I said casually.

It was after dinner, when the children were in bed that the questions started. "How are you doing, Mum? Any luck with the job hunt?"

"Oh, I have a few leads." My stomach tightened. If he knew the truth about my circumstances, he would insist on giving me money and then I'd be dependent on him.

Amy said, "Did Jason tell you that you're welcome to stay with us?"

"Yes he did, Amy. Thank you, but I like living alone."

"We could make a suite in the basement. You could sell your house, live off the proceeds, and you wouldn't have to work." Amy sat back and smiled like an evangelical pastor.

I took a deep breath. "Thank you, Amy, but I value my independence." Keep calm. They are only trying to be helpful. They want what's best for me.

Jason and Amy exchanged glances. Jason said, "The suite would be your private place. We wouldn't allow the children in."

"I know you both mean well, but no, I do not want to move. I'm fine. I have a house and I have enough money. Now, can we talk about something else?" I stared out of the window. Jason cleared his throat. Amy fiddled with things on the tea tray.

"I do like the lighter evenings, don't you?" I said.

"It will soon be warm enough to sit outside," Amy said. She offered me a plate. "Another cookie? They're delicious." What she would say if I told her the ingredients came from the food bank?

There was silence for a while and then Amy said, "We had some excitement here the other day. There was a bust at the house across the road."

"A bust?" I didn't know what she meant.

"A bust of a grow-op."

I must have looked blank. Jason said, "You know, Mum. A grow-op is when people grow pot, marijuana, in their basement."

My skin prickled. "Oh."

"Amy figured it out. She saw something suspicious and phoned the police." He flushed slightly and wouldn't look at me. What did he really think about neighbors snitching on each other? At one time he would have been disgusted.

"What did you see, Amy?" I asked. Whatever she saw I must be careful to take note.

"It was dark but they had their garage open and lit, so I could see everything. They were unloading bales of soil and loading a lot of garbage bags into a truck."

"Isn't this the time of year for bales of soil?"

"At night? No, I wasn't sure but I phoned the police with my suspicions. And I was right!" Amy finished, looking smug.

Jason and I didn't say anything. "Grow-ops are a real problem in this town," Amy went on.

"I can't see what the problem is," I said. "There's very little crime."

"No. But there could be," Amy said. "I can't believe I ever let the children play over there. I've been inside houses that had grow-ops to assess childrens' safety."

"What were they like?"

"Dangerous. Hazards everywhere. One had lights in the living room with naked wires all ready to start a fire. In the living room! Another one had the lights in the basement, but mold in the walls. You wouldn't believe how some people live." Amy shook her head vigorously. "Imagine bringing up children in scenes like that."

I changed the subject by asking about Julie's toilet training. If I did decide to start growing—don't unload bales of soil at night, get rid of garbage in small loads, make sure the neighbors can't see—I would have to be very, very careful. If Amy ever found out what I was thinking of, I might lose my family. I wasn't sure about Jason. But Amy had seen grow-ops and obviously thought they were evil. Maybe they were. I didn't know.

In a funny way it was the thought of Amy's horror that spurred me to make the phone call to Marcus.

8

I WAITED at the window for Marcus to arrive, expecting him to be late. But no, his old battered truck drew up promptly at nine. I was in a dither, pulling on my ear lobe continually and getting up and down from my chair, unable to settle. Would my basement be suitable? Would he be able to set me up as Swan said he would? But most of all, was this a wise move?

Marcus unfolded himself out of his truck, reached inside for a few things, and started up my front path. He really was a great gawk with his gangly legs and huge hands and feet. He held a paper cup of coffee in front of him as if it might slop down his front, but still managed to walk as if his jeans were too tight for his family jewels.

I opened the door before he had time to ring and said, "Hi Marcus. Come in." I couldn't stop myself looking up and down the street before closing the door.

I hadn't seen Marcus since the day of the fire. He stood, staring at the floor, running a finger round the rim of his cup.

I had a chance to study him. An impassive face, clean-shaven except for the soul patch, not handsome but not unpleasant; a face you wouldn't fall over yourself to greet. He was strangely silent. I had the urge to say, "Has the cat got your tongue," like my mother used to. Not that he made me feel motherly, but I did want to sit him down in front of a good fry-up to fill him out a bit.

"You want to look at my basement?" I asked.

"Yep."

"Don't take your shoes off," I said, though he had made no move to do so. "This way."

I led him through a door in the hall, down the steep wooden steps into what I thought of as an underground fusty cavern with spiders and other unseen creepy crawlies. It's a cavern I only visited to do laundry, re-light the furnace when it went out, or find out if the hot water tank had leaked. On the way down, Marcus knocked over a can of paint that was stored on a shelf beside the stairs. He didn't bend down to pick it up. I did. No "sorry" or comment.

I turned on the two dim lights. Marcus put his coffee cup down on the washing machine and looked around. He inspected the old stone sink and tried the tap, which spat out water in small bursts. "Get this fixed," he grunted.

Someone had once built a long, shelf-lined cupboard, probably for storing canned fruit and root vegetables but that I used for garden tools and oddments. "Hmm," Marcus said as he opened its door.

"Will that be useful?" I asked.

Marcus gave the first of many irritating shrugs. He then turned his attention to the ceiling, particularly to the round hole that a wood stove had once been vented through. "Got a screwdriver?" he said. Three words.

My tools were in the storage cupboard and while I searched, Marcus stood on a stool and fiddled with the wooden cover of the hole. I handed him my set of screwdrivers. He selected one and handed the rest back. Although his hands were huge, his fingers were long and agile and the cover was off in a moment. He stepped off the stool quickly as a pile of mouse droppings and black dust fell on the floor. "Know where this goes?" Four words.

"Straight up to the roof, I think." I had once inspected the various chimneys when I had my living room gas fire installed and had to have the main chimney re-lined.

"Good," Marcus said.

"Don't take my word for it," I added hastily. He didn't answer but opened the back door leading into the garden, and looked out. "Where's your panel?" he said as he closed the door.

"What panel?"

"Electric."

"Upstairs." I'd have to practice terse sentences if I decided to spend time with him.

I headed for the stairs, but Marcus had produced a tape measure and a used envelope and was measuring the large, empty space that held trunks and boxes. "Move those," he said, pointing to them.

"Right," I said.

"Hold that." Marcus handed me one end of the tape measure. "Against that wall." He wrote down the measurements on the envelope while I held the tape.

"Will it be suitable?" I asked as he finally retracted the measure. I was half hoping he would say "no" so I could forget the whole idea.

"You'll see." He gave a final look around and made for the stairs. I followed. "Panel?" he said at the top.

I showed him the panel in the hall.

"Get another."

"Another what?"

"Another panel. Get an electrician. And a dryer outlet."

"Where shall I ask him to put them?" I said.

Marcus had his hand on the front door knob. "Downstairs."

"Whereabouts?" I called as he marched down the path.

He shrugged.

I wanted to throw something at him, but I went downstairs to turn off the lights and fetch his coffee cup. Even if the basement turned out to be suitable for a grow-op, I wasn't sure I could handle Marcus on a regular basis. He didn't seem very competent. And he certainly wasn't forthcoming. Yet Swan thought he knew what he was doing. Supposing he didn't? What if he didn't wire the lights properly and my house went up in flames? Insurance doesn't cover you if a fire is the result of an illegal activity.

I made myself a cup of tea. I could hardly believe that I was seriously considering a grow-op in my basement. Me—a person who never smuggles things over the border, never cheats on my income tax, always points out a cashier's error in my favor. I might end up in jail! What would I look like in orange overalls and a little headscarf?

I told myself to stop it; lots of people in Nelson grow

marijuana. I would simply be joining a different group. I would no longer call myself a waitress. "What do you do, Jess?" "Oh, I have some growing investments." Anyway, even if I didn't know if Marcus could set me up, it wouldn't do any harm to put another electrical panel in the house. I might be able to rent the space to a potter.

I reached for the Yellow Pages to look for an electrician. Then I had second thoughts. What was I going to ask him to do and why? I didn't know where another panel should go, or a dryer outlet. And what explanation would I give about why I needed them? I phoned Swan instead and left a message for her to call me.

Swan came round the following evening. This time she had a tuft of blue hair springing straight up from her head so that she looked all the world like a blue jay—a blue jay with a bit of metal in its lip and black around its eyes.

I told her about Marcus's visit. "He doesn't explain *any-thing*," I said. "He wants me to put in another electrical panel and a dryer outlet, but where? I can't ask an electrician to come if I can't say what I want. Or why."

Swan tugged at the cuffs of her black sweater, one with arms that would fit an ape, and drew the sleeves over her hands. "Let's go down to the basement."

"Hmm, nice space," she said when we reached the foot of the steps. She turned on the water at the sink. "Need a new tap. One that will take a hose."

She wandered around and looked in the storage cupboard.

"That will be useful. He'll probably make the door to the room here." She indicated the corner of the cupboard. "But I don't know. Just let him do it."

"Room?" I said. "Doesn't he use this space." I waved my arm round the basement.

"Yeah. But he'll build a room in it. You'll see." She looked at the hole in the ceiling.

"He was very interested in that," I said.

"That's where the duct pipe will go."

"What duct pipe?"

Swan looked at me pityingly and shook her head. "Jess, a grow room has to have several things: lights—big ones— air intake, air exit, and something to control the smell." She waved at the main space. "This is where the lights will go. You've got room for four. I'm not sure where he'll put the intake duct, but the exit will go through this old chimney. Sweet."

Swan opened the door to the cupboard again. "Your watering bin will go in here. And your seedlings." She patted a shelf. "He'll probably fit up fluorescent lights for them. Awesome. No waiting between crops."

Swan spoke with such authority I could hardly believe it.

"Don't let him give you Skunk plants. They stink." She walked around the space toward the back door.

"I can't tell a marijuana plant from a dandelion so I wouldn't know. Do they all stink?"

"Some. A good filter helps."

By this time I was thinking I'd bitten off more than I could chew. I hadn't really thought about what was involved. I had imagined a few plant pots in the basement, that's all, not a whole room, *a grow room*. Suppose someone came downstairs and saw a room? Jason, or Amy? What would I do when I needed the furnace serviced?

I was about to tell Swan to forget it, I couldn't do this, when she opened the back door and stepped out. It was dark and she couldn't see much. "Can you use the lane?"

"Yes. My garage is there."

"Wicked."

Back inside, Swan said, "I'd put the dryer outlet here." She indicated a spot half way along the wall of the main space. "You'll have to move all those boxes." She walked over to the furnace and hot water tank. "And I'd put the panel here," she said, pointing to the wall at the foot of the stairs.

"How am I going to pay for them? I'm broke."

"Give the bill to Marcus. He'll pay it. You'll pay him back at the end." Swan moved to the middle of the room and slowly looked around.

"What shall I say I need them for?"

"You don't have to explain."

"I can't ask an electrician to come and put in a new panel and a outlet without saying why," I said.

"Tell him you're reno-ing the kitchen and you need more power. And you're getting a dryer down here. You've only got that old washer, right? In fact, get him to put in two dryer outlets in case you do get a dryer."

I nodded. I hung out my washing on lines strung across the basement. Maybe I'd be able to afford a new washer and dryer. That would be wonderful.

"Move these but keep 'em." Swan pulled on a line. "You'll need 'em for drying the weed."

I looked at her with new eyes. She'd turned into my teacher, someone to help me with a new way of life, a conspirator. I gave her a spontaneous hug. "Thanks, Swan. I don't feel quite so lost."

She hugged me back. "No prob. I'll come and help you whenever you want. Marcus isn't a talker, in case you hadn't noticed. Head injury, you know. Climbing accident. Tragic."

As Swan was about to leave, she said, "I nearly forgot, Marcus needs a key so he can get in when he wants."

"You mean he can come in and wander around the house when he feels like it?"

Swan gave me her 'seriously?' look again. "Jess, he isn't going to rob you. Or attack you. Of course he has to get in."

"Even when he's finished setting up?"

"He isn't just setting you up. There'll be the plants to look after and all sorts of things to check."

"Don't I do that?"

"Do you know how?"

I shook my head. "Of course not."

"You're going to need lots of help. A back door key would be best. Then he can park his truck out there. Do you have a spare key?"

I found a key and a key ring and gave them to Swan. "Will you be seeing Marcus?"

"Yep."

She had said he wasn't her boyfriend, but they seemed to see a lot of each other.

"Call him when the electrician's finished," she said as she left. "And you can always lock the inside door to the basement, if you're worried."

I leaned on the front door after I'd closed it. What on earth was I doing? I nearly called after Swan "Stop. I can't go through with this," but I didn't. The half of me that was gleeful, the half that I always subdued, took over. This was the most exhilarating thing that had ever happened to me.

In the living room I played Abba. "Take a chance on me," I sang as I danced around. "Take a chance on me-e-e."

9

THE NEXT MEETING of the Crones was held at Ainsworth Hot Springs. Should I go? The entry fee had gone up and I would have to pitch in for gas. To hell with it. I need this. I'll skip a meal tomorrow.

As usual on outings we met at Extra Foods, ready to be picked up by the two women who had volunteered to drive. Not many Crones drove any more, either because they didn't feel able, or—more likely—they couldn't afford a car. It was more a question of who was available to drive rather than who would.

Eva didn't come on outings. She was too much of a liability, as she tended to wander off. So her poor husband didn't get the two-hour respite he enjoyed when we had our meetings at the church.

This time there were six of us traveling in two cars, one driven by Maggie and one by Joan. I was with Laura in Maggie's car and although Maggie tried to maneuver me into the front seat, she was beaten to it by Laura, who simply piled in. This meant that Maggie was the recipient of Laura's medical news. I was glad to settle in the back so I could avoid conversation. I wanted this break to help me simmer down and think things through, not get worked up over other people's problems. Life was in control of me, not the other way round, and I was hurtling toward something I didn't necessarily want.

"Now, would you believe it, my cholesterol is up!" Laura exclaimed. "As if I don't have enough to put up with."

"Easily controlled by diet," Maggie said as she turned onto Nelson Avenue.

"Yes, the doctor says I have to control my diet, but he's also put me on statins. That should do it." Laura settled into her seat.

Maggie groaned. "I suppose I'm wasting my breath if I tell you how dangerous they are?"

"My doctor wouldn't prescribe them if they were dangerous."

"He wouldn't, eh?"

There was silence for a while. When Laura realized Maggie wasn't going to continue, she said, "Why are they dangerous?"

"Statins work by acting on an enzyme in the liver. But they also block important nutrients that you need for a healthy heart. So they're counter-productive."

"He told me they would prevent me having a heart attack."

I couldn't see Maggie's face, but I expect she had her "bullshit" look on.

Laura twisted in her seat to look at me. "What do you think, Jess?"

"About what?" I didn't want to get into that discussion.

"About cholesterol."

"All I know is that whenever there's a big song and dance about anything, like cholesterol or bone density, my crap detector starts to vibrate."

"So you don't believe in cholesterol?" Laura turned to face the front again.

I rolled my eyes. "Cholesterol isn't something you *believe* in. What I do believe is that I'm in charge of my health, not a doctor, and that they don't know everything."

"Oh."

Now, maybe, we could move on. "The lake looks lovely today," I said. "Almost summery." I loved the drive along Kootenay Lake and the views of the mountains, that still had snow on the peaks, and the trees taking on their summer leaves. It's the sort of view that people travel thousands of miles to see in other countries but that we had on our doorstep.

"I don't want to have a heart attack or a stroke," Laura whined.

"Neither does anyone else," Maggie said. "Laura, if your doctor told you to live in a wheelchair to prevent heart attacks, would you do it?"

"No, of course not."

"Why not?"

"I don't need a wheelchair."

"Exactly." Maggie slowed for road works. An older woman held up a STOP sign. Could it be Nancy? Was she back on the job?

"Jess, how's the job hunting coming along? Weren't

you going to look into this?" Maggie indicated the traffic controller.

"I did inquire about this job," I said, "but you have to take a course that costs two hundred dollars. Which I don't have."

"You'd want to do *that*?" Laura asked.

"Not particularly. But it pays twelve bucks an hour."

"I'd hate it. Standing in fumes all day and out in all weather," Laura said dismissively.

"We can't all do what we want," Maggie said as we headed off again. "Or I'd be a naturopath."

"What do you need to do to become one?" Maggie had never said that was her ambition. She had studied plants and their medicinal uses and had taken a course in homeopathy, but she hadn't mentioned naturopathy. Wasn't she too old now?

"I'd have to go to college for four years. But I'm saving up." She smiled at me through the rear-view mirror. "One day. Before I'm too old."

The first step into the delicious warmth of the hot springs made all my cells relax and get ready to enjoy the influx of minerals from the water. A feeling of peace swept over me. I started off in the hottest pool where I could close my eyes and think, while everyone else was in the cooler pool.

I'd really done it now. There was no going back. Marcus had been hammering away in the basement and I now had another room in my house. A grow room. I was in a movie and I would shortly go to a dressing room, take off my costume and come out as Jess. The old Jess. The sober, upright, hard-working waitress.

Now what was I? A criminal, that's what I was. Oh, get off it. You're just the same. You're doing something you've never done before, that's all. It's exciting, that's what it is. A new venture; one that will give you some money. Yeah. And now I had a secret. The last time I had a secret was at school when Jeannie Robertson and I spent our dinner money on pork pies and cigarettes, which we ate and smoked in the local park. I wish I had someone to share my secret with, other than Marcus and Swan, someone I could exchange knowing glances with or discuss types of marijuana and how to grow them.

What was the worst that could happen? I could go to jail. Then I wouldn't have to worry about money. I would be kept in relative comfort but behind bars, that's all. I could get on with my cross-stitch and knitting. I'd end up with a criminal record, but so what at my age? Better than ending up as a starving bag lady who had to use food banks.

Feeling better, I entered the cooler pool and joined the others who had gathered in one recess. Claire was tugging at the crotch of her swimsuit. "I just got this from the Thrift Shop. But it's not long enough. It's catching my pubic hair."

"You're lucky to still have pubic hair," Jane said.

"It's thinned a lot," Claire admitted. "I used to be so proud of my bush."

"My husband loved stroking mine. Now it feels like a scrubbing brush," Joan said.

"Are you two still at it?"

"Once in a while. Not like the old days, that's for sure." Joan sank lower in the water and sat on the bench. "Now I have to tell him that if I die before he comes, he should pull my nightie down."

We all grinned. Joan and Thelma were the only ones, besides Eva, who still had a husband.

"It's me that gets the urge, not him," Joan continued. "What do you guys do when you get that urge? Or have you given up?"

"I take care of myself," I said. After Frank and I split up the need drove me crazy and eventually I learned how to relieve it.

"How?" Jane asked.

"I don't talk about that in a hot spring." I sank under the water for a moment.

"I use a dildo," Jane announced as if she were telling us she used a fork instead of a whisk to beat eggs.

Joan was clearly amazed. "Where did you get it?"

"There used to be a shop in Nelson. It's gone now, but you can get them on the Internet. You wouldn't believe the shapes and colors."

I had never seen Jane as an expert on sex toys. You learn something new about people every day.

"I've looked at those," Claire said. "There's one that's purple and fifteen inches long, can you believe it?"

"You could do yourself a mischief," I said.

"Do they sell male enhancement pills?" Joan asked. "I'd like to get some for Ted."

"I don't know," Jane said. "I've never needed them."

"What the hell are male enhancement pills?" Claire laid back in the water.

"They give men a better hard on," Joan said. "Believe me, Ted needs them."

All this time Laura had not said a word. In her swimsuit

she looked thinner than ever; haggard, in fact. If she took herself off all her drugs and dried out, would she be any better? A geriatric nurse once told me that's what they do when old people are first admitted to a nursing home. Many of them perk right up.

"That young couple over there might have overheard every word we've said," Claire whispered.

"Oh, I do hope so," I said loudly.

10

THE BASEMENT BECAME a cave, a cave of possibilities, a secret cave where treasures were to be found, no longer a fusty cavern. An electrician had installed another panel and two dryer outlets without comment, and I had humped the storage boxes up into the spare room so that everything was ready for Marcus.

I hadn't been in when he first visited. The clues were rolls of plastic, two by fours, insulation, and a toolbox lying by the back door. He came and went, but never talked to me, asked me what I wanted, or reviewed his progress. So the first time I saw the room he had built, I stood with my mouth open. I reached the bottom step and didn't know where I was—the whole basement had changed shape. The old sink, washing machine, hot water tank and furnace were still clustered to my left, the outside door was still straight ahead, but to my right ran a wall made of wooden joists with pink insulation between them and covered with heavy clear plastic. The door to the cupboard, near the foot of the stairs, gave entry.

I opened the door, but it was so dark I had to go back upstairs for a flashlight. With it I located the utility light hanging from a nail and switched it on. The original cupboard was much the same and formed the entrance, like a foyer, to a room on my left, accessed through a flap of heavy plastic fastened with Velcro. I opened the flap, stepped over a two by four support and entered a room lined with white plastic that reflected the light on me to form a giant shadow. I made a duck with my hands and quacked it along the wall before inspecting the small slots made for numerous electric outlets and the large slot for the dryer outlet. The ceiling, also covered with white plastic, had a solid piece of wood nailed across its entire length, with four black crosses marked on it.

No sign of Marcus. I was determined to interact with him, so when I heard his truck the next day, I hurried downstairs. He was unloading strange metal objects, objects that I couldn't identify, and piling them in the space next to the back door.

"Good morning," I said.

He grunted, walked out to return a few seconds later with two evidently heavy metal boxes.

"What are those?" I asked.

"Ballasts."

"What's a ballast?"

"For the lights."

"What do they do?"

"Control the current." Marcus stood awkwardly beside his pile of equipment until I realized I was blocking his path into the room. I moved to the foot of the stairs, out of the way, as he carried things into the old cupboard.

"Would you like a cup of coffee?" I said.

"Thanks."

Did this mean No, thanks, or Yes, please? I went up to make coffee because I wanted an excuse to go down again. When I returned with a filled mug and a cookie, Marcus had gone.

I had been out of work for more than three months and had been meaning to tackle a list of 'to do's' but I never had the energy, not even enough to start knitting a sweater for Nicholas. I had the wool and the pattern, but I never felt like it. Now the activity in the basement inspired me to action and I decided to clean out my bedroom closets.

There's no mound of cushions on my bed, no ornaments in the room, no frilly drapes. What's the point of the cushions some people stack on their beds? You only have to take them off to get into bed and then where do you put them? The duvet cover of bright red poppies cheered the room, and me. Field poppies grow everywhere in England, especially along the sides of country lanes. As kids we used to make dolls with them—we folded down the petals to make a skirt and wrapped a piece of grass around to hold it in place. The stamen became the head.

Oh good grief! Poppies made opium. Is that why I liked them? Did I have some unknown longing for drugs? Is that why I wanted to grow pot? I shook my head hard. Stop being so daft and get on with clearing out.

My closets were cupboards built under the eaves of the

old house, not real closets. I didn't even know what was in them any more. I spotted the weights that I bought when I was going to turn into a Strong Woman, the elastic straps for turning into a Flexible Woman, and the jogging shoes when I was going to train my dickey heart to allow me to bound up mountains without a gasp.

Work clothes—obtained from thrift stores—occupied most of the space. I never wore skirts any more. Women didn't wear pants when I grew up, and as a schoolgirl I suffered from cold legs all the time. We wore knee socks, for heaven's sake. My very first pair of trousers was made of tartan wool and I still remembered their warmth and how easy it was to move in them. For years I'd worn pants all the time, but not jeans. I could never find any that fit me and the legs were always at least twelve inches too long. Besides, jeans and white hair don't go together.

My bedroom window looked out across to Elephant Mountain and down onto the back lane. Marcus's truck was parked beside the garage. I hadn't heard him come in. Thoughts of clearing out closets vanished as I hurried downstairs.

In the basement cupboard, a new shelf supported four ballasts with a bungee cord around each one and attached to sturdy hooks. A strange gray metal box with a dial on it was screwed to the far wall. What was that for? I peered into the grow room. Four large, gleaming lampshades lay on the floor like giant silver water lilies, and numerous thick wires squirmed around them. A tall cylinder stood in the far corner and from it extended a concertinaed tube that ran out through a new hole in top of the wall.

Marcus paused from screwing metal plates into the ceiling of the room. "Come back in fifteen," he said.

Up in my bedroom I took clothes out of one closet, stared at them, and either put them back or folded them into the donation bag. Time moved very slowly, but eventually fifteen minutes passed and I could go downstairs.

The first thing I saw when I reached the foot of the basement stairs was the silver concertinaed tube, about ten inches wide, running across the ceiling and up through the chimney hole. It couldn't have been more obvious—anyone coming downstairs would see it instantly.

"Bloody hell," I said out loud.

Marcus emerged from the cupboard and stood holding a length of rope as if he didn't know what to do next.

"Does that have to be so obvious?" I said, pointing to the tube.

He stared at me with expressionless eyes.

"I mean, anyone who walks in would see it at once," I continued.

He shrugged before slinging the rope around the tube and tying it to a hook in the ceiling. It did raise the tube, but did nothing to hide it.

"Lights are ready," he said.

We passed through the flap into the grow room. Three long, narrow light bulbs and one big round one hung down from under huge silver shades. I had never seen such large bulbs—or shades.

Marcus pushed a lever on the gray box, the ballasts started to hum, and each bulb took on a glow. "Don't look at the lights as they come on," Marcus said.

"Why not?" My first instruction from him surprised me. "Makes you blind."

It took a few minutes before the lights glowed fully and I was able to look in the room. The brightness made me blink. "I'm going to need sunglasses," I said.

Marcus bent down to adjust another concertinaed tube that ran along the floor, into a fan and from that out through a hole into the cupboard. It ended up going through a hole in the far side of the cupboard. "What's that?" I asked.

"Air vent." He pointed to the gray box. "Timer."

"Timer?"

A nod.

"What for?"

"The lights."

I needed Swan to visit and explain how all these devices worked. Marcus switched off the lights and the noise from the ballasts stopped.

"I had no idea those things would make so much noise," I said. "Is there any way to reduce it?"

Marcus shrugged and spread his hands. "You want two- or three-gallon pots?"

"What difference does it make?"

"More plants with two-gallon. Fewer but bigger with three-gallon."

"What do you think?"

He shrugged.

"I'll talk to Swan and tell you later."

A message on my voice mail asked me to call Maggie. She told me that Laura was in the hospital. "No one seems to know what's wrong with her," Maggie said. "She can't stand up and she can't walk. So she's in having tests."

"Oh dear," I said. "I thought she looked awful at the hot springs. Thin as a rail."

"That's the other thing, she's not eating. Anyway, I thought I'd let you know in case you want to go and see her."

"I'll go up there this evening," I said.

"I'm coming into town on Thursday. I'll pop in then and take her some flowers from my garden. Let me know how she is if you do visit."

"Will do."

I didn't really want to visit Laura because she was one long moan. She had every ailment that was currently fashionable, like osteopenia. Maggie had told her there's no such disease, that it was made up by the pharmaceutical industry, but she ignored her; she only believed her doctor. I found her very hard to bear—I always wanted to shake her and tell her to snap out of it and do something useful with her life.

Swan was coming over after work. I looked at the time; if I went to the hospital right away I would be back for Swan. I wouldn't be able to stay long and I'd have an excuse to leave. To be honest, I was far too engrossed in my new venture to pay attention to Laura, but I like to feel loyal to the Crones, so I went.

Laura lay between sheets that matched her pallor and held out a bony hand to me. "Good of you to come, Jess," she said in a weak little voice that I had to strain to hear. "Looks like the devil is winning." She attempted a smile.

"What's happened?" I put the small plant I'd brought on the windowsill.

"The doctor gave me pills for this and that, but nothing seemed to help. Then gradually I got so I couldn't walk; now I can't even stand without holding on to something." Laura reached weakly for her glass of water. I jumped up to help and held the glass to her lips.

"They think it's neurological," she said after taking a sip. "I'm to have blood tests and they're taking me to Trail to see a neurologist."

"The neurologist can't come here?"

"I guess not."

"Is there anything I can do?"

Laura stared at me with pale, watery eyes. "Thank you, Jess, but Monica next door is feeding the cat and will bring me anything I need. She's very good that way."

"Would you like something to read?" I asked, as there were no books to be seen. "A magazine, a puzzle book, or something? It must be pretty boring staring at the curtains."

"Oh, I haven't the energy to read. I can't even hold up a book."

"Would you like me to get you one of those talking books they have at the library?" I persisted. "They have them on neat little players that come with head phones."

"My hearing isn't very good."

I gave up, chatted about the weather, and left.

True to her word, Swan showed up on her way home from work. She looked all scrubbed and clean with short, unpainted fingernails, no straggly hair, but her eyes were heavily made up as usual. I supposed she'd had to clean herself up because she worked in a deli. She seemed impressed when she saw the basement. "Wow, that was quick. This is epic."

I pointed at the duct tube. "That's a big giveaway."

"No biggie. All you have to do is fold it away if someone comes down. Look." She climbed up on a stool and pulled the tube out of the chimney hole. "See, it comes out easy. Just undo that rope and fold it through the hole into the room. Marcus probably left the piece he cut out somewhere. Yep, there it is." She pushed the tube back into the chimney, climbed down and picked up a round piece of insulation. "This'll cover the hole and then just fold the plastic back over it."

"What does it do anyway?" I asked. "Is it really necessary?"

"It's attached to the filter to get rid of the smell. So, yeah, you need it."

Without the duct tube the basement would look normal to someone who hadn't seen it before. To someone who knew what it used to be like I could say I had built a storeroom that I could rent out. But then, no one who visited me ever wanted to go in the basement. Come to think of it, I never expected to enter anyone else's basement unless they had a room in it they used, like Jason's office.

Swan moved through the door into the cupboard and switched on the light Marcus had put in there. "Neat," she said. "You can put a row of strip lights in here for cuttings and there's plenty of storage space for food and whatever."

"What cuttings?"

"You always have a couple of plants growing to provide babies for the next grow." She peered through the flap into the grow room. "Can I turn the lights on?"

"Please do," I said. "Marcus said you go blind if you watch them come on. Is that right?"

"I don't think you'd go blind, but it doesn't do your eyes any good."

The ballasts began to hum and the lights came on. Swan entered the room and strolled around the perimeter. "Lots of room to water." She took hold of the chain holding one light and lengthened it by hanging it from another link. "This is how you raise and lower the light."

"Why would I want to do that?"

"You really are a newbie, aren't you? The lights have to be about eighteen inches from the plants, so when they're little the lights are low and as they grow you raise them."

"Oh, I see. I think I can manage that."

"Let me show you the timer." Swan moved into the cupboard and pointed at the gray box. "This dial sets the time. These levers set when the lights come on and go off. When the plants are in veg they need eighteen hours of light and six hours of dark. Then when they're in grow they need twelve hours of light and twelve hours of dark."

I didn't understand, but by then I was too befuddled to ask. I needed my glasses to see the dial on the timer and figure out how it worked, so I'd have to come back later.

Swan pointed to the small levers that indicated the time for off and on. "Make sure these are tight. Sometimes they slip so the lights stay on or off all the time."

"I wish those ballasts didn't make that noise," I said.

"Let's go upstairs and see if we can hear them," Swan said. She closed the flap, the cupboard door, and the door down to the basement. In the kitchen I could still hear the hum, faint though it was.

"I can hear it up here," I said. "Anyone coming in would hear it."

"Nah, people don't notice house sounds. I wouldn't hear it if I didn't know it was there. Could be the fridge; anything. Gotta fly. I'll come by tomorrow."

"Oh, before you go, should I use two-gallon or three-gallon pots? Marcus asked me what I wanted."

"I'd go for two-gallons. They're lighter for you to carry and don't use as much soil. Some people think the plants are bigger in three-gallons." Swan started to move toward the front door. "But two-gallons do need watering more. You could try both and see."

I found a spare pair of glasses and took them down to leave in my secret room. The timer seemed quite simple, but the screws were too tiny for my thick fingers to turn so I searched for thin pliers. I practised setting the timer with the pliers. There. That wasn't difficult. You can do it.

11

MY OTHER LIFE took over on Sunday when I went for dinner with the family. I should have had a switch inside me, like the light timer switches, that turned to Real Jess on one setting and Criminal Jess on the other. As I drove to Jason's house I switched to Real Jess.

Nicholas and I had played a game on my previous visit, so he was waiting for me when I arrived, eager to do the same. We were to walk round the garden picking fruit from imaginary trees or pretending to dig for vegetables.

"I can't reach that pear, Nicholas," I said, stretching an arm up toward the sky. "If I lift you up, can you get it?" I held him in the air and he grabbed at nothing. "What a beautiful pear; it's almost ripe. Now, how about some oranges?"

When our baskets were full we joined the family on the patio.

Nicholas offered a make-believe squash to Jason who stopped poking meat on the barbecue, opened his arms, bent double to hold the pretend weight, and thanked Nicholas with enthusiasm. At least one parent encouraged his son's imagination. Amy probably saw it as a disorder—reality avoidance disorder or some such nonsense.

Jason and Amy had stopped talking about my living with them, thank heaven. They were engrossed in renovations of their laundry room, which they hoped to finish before they left for a month's summer holiday on the Sunshine Coast.

"Are you planning to get away, Mum?" Jason asked.

"Just day trips," I said. "Maybe next year."

"When did you last visit Britain?"

"Hmm. Five, maybe six, years ago." I took a sip of wine. "I don't know anyone there now, except Vera, and she's crippled with arthritis."

"You should go anyway," Amy said. "Explore your roots."

"My roots were dug up years ago. Rotted by now. But I wouldn't mind a visit to York and the Dales."

I could see myself on a luxury coach, sitting high, admiring the gentle heather-covered slopes of Wharfedale, the dry stone walls dividing fields into patchwork, the stone barns with slate roofs, the river Wharfe meandering by, the bleat of sheep, hikers carefully closing gates after themselves, the sweet smell of the heather—the sweetest smell in the world. Maybe my buddies would take me there next year.

"If I was going to fly anywhere," I continued, "I'd like to visit Lisa. She's been saying I should go, but it's such a long way."

"You could rent out your house if you go for a few months," Jason said. "That would help with expenses."

"If I did go to New Zealand I wouldn't have hotel expenses. Lisa has a spare room and she said that if I do visit she would take time off and drive me round. That would be nice."

"Does she ever talk about coming home?" Amy asked.

"She thinks of New Zealand as her home now." I sighed. "I do miss her. I long for her letters, but she doesn't have much time to write."

"I really must get you a computer, Mum," Jason said. "But would you use it?"

"I'm warming to the idea. They had some training sessions at the library to show us how to use theirs. It doesn't seem too difficult. But it's when something goes wrong I wouldn't know what to do."

"Not many people do. That's where nerds like me come in. To set you up and troubleshoot. You would like one then?" Jason smiled.

I nodded.

Swan had obviously talked to Marcus because when I came home from my now routine visit to the food bank, there was a stack of two-gallon plant pots and three bales of soil piled up near the back door.

A rubber garden hose snaked across the floor from the new tap on the sink. I followed it into the cupboard where it ended up in a giant garbage pail. Another hose, attached to what I assumed was a pump at the bottom of the pail, ran out into the grow room and connected to a watering wand.

Four pedestal fans were stacked in one corner of the room and a new gauge had appeared on one wall. I took my hat off to Marcus—he definitely wasted no time.

All this activity suggested I should do something, but what? Should I fill the pots with soil? I felt useless, but I was so afraid of doing something wrong that I couldn't do anything at all. I was just about to go upstairs and vacuum when the back door key turned and Marcus backed in dragging a couple of wooden pallets. He didn't see me so he startled when I said, "Wow, you've been busy."

He turned around and leaned the pallets against the wall. "To put the plant pots on," he said, nodding at the pallets. Then, to my astonishment, he added more words, "Plants get cold straight on the concrete floor." I must have looked dumbfounded because he repeated, staring at me as if I were a particularly slow schoolchild, "Plants get cold when they're straight on the concrete floor."

He went out again and came back immediately with another two pallets, which he dragged into the grow room.

He wore shorts that allowed a view of solid, muscular legs with the bulging calves of a cyclist. Or a rock climber. If I had been thirty years younger…

In the grow room, where he was arranging the pallets, one under each light, I said, "I was thinking I should fill the plant pots with soil. Right?"

He looked down at me, his face in shadow from the utility light. I thought I saw his eyes gleam. "If you do that, I'll bring the plants tonight. After dark."

"How many? I mean, how many pots shall I fill?"

"Thirty-two two-gallons and two three-gallons for the mothers."

"Right," I said. *Mothers?* I didn't understand but I didn't want to push my luck when Marcus was so surprisingly vocal.

I could hardly eat my boiled spuds. What would the plants look like? I couldn't tell the difference between a marijuana plant and a chrysanthemum. All I knew was that they smelled, but Swan had said it was a different smell from the one when people smoked. Would they live in my house? What if they just shrivelled and died?

I changed into an old jogging suit and descended into the depths. Like so many packages these days, the damned bales of soil were hermetically sealed. Back upstairs for kitchen scissors. I cut open the plastic and revealed a solid mass of peaty earth that I attacked with a trowel. Much of it did go into the pots but even more fell on the floor. There had to be a better way of doing this job. Next time I would scrape the soil into a storage bin, loosen it, and then fill the pots.

It was warm work bending down shoveling soil into pots. I would have opened the door, but what if someone saw me? Eventually, after sweat began to drip off my face, common sense told me to open the door. The breeze was delicious.

Between my door and the house opposite lay my small garden, my garage, the lane, another garage, another garden, and finally, a house with windows. Anyone at the upper windows would be able to see my door but not inside it. Marcus's truck, when parked in the space next to the garage, would block even that view. I stopped worrying that someone would have seen him unload.

A young working couple occupied the house directly across the lane and they were in so rarely that they wouldn't see me. It was their neighbor who might cause trouble. I didn't know her terribly well—just to say "hello" to—but Kate was a vigorous, single woman in her fifties who had a lot to say about a lot of subjects. If there was a report in the paper about the Health Cooperative, there was her name; if there was a picture of a group presenting a check to buy the community a mini-bus, there was her picture. If anyone would snitch on me, it would be her.

Eventually two long lines of filled plant pots ran alongside the outer wall of the grow room. I carried them into the room and arranged eight on each pallet. The lights, of course, were off and the utility light lit the room. Now I needed to add water to the pots as I knew from experience with potting houseplants that new soil with perlite in it takes ages to absorb water.

The large garbage bin was obviously meant as a reservoir so I filled it by simply turning the tap at the sink. So far, so good. Now, how was the water to reach the wand? With the pump, of course. I'm not good at mechanical things, so I was proud of myself when I discovered the switch for the pump, pressed the handle of the wand, and watched the water come out.

Swan was right; it was easy to walk round the room and squirt water into the pots but then, as pools began to form on the floor, I realized the pots needed saucers. The storage area near the back door was void of saucers but I did discover two three-gallon pots. Marcus had said they were for the mothers but who were the mothers? I filled them with soil anyway and left them where they were.

That was all I could do, so then I had to wait. I made macaroni and cheese from a package and ate it in front of the television, picked up my knitting, put it down again, washed up, turned the television to another station, then another, knitted three rows and finally, in exasperation, wandered into the front garden to do some weeding.

It was like waiting for Christmas as a child and just as exciting, except I knew what the parcel would contain. At least, I knew it would be plants, but what would they look like? How big? I began to feel tender toward them before I'd even seen them; my little buddies to nurture and care for; little buddies who would grow up and look after me in my old age.

A neighbor walked past and wished me a good evening. Both the houses on either side of me were rented: usually to students, usually young and transient, usually noisy. It wouldn't occur to them that an old biddy like me would grow pot and if it did, they would probably want to help.

When I thought my nervous system would collapse under the strain of anticipation, Swan knocked on the front door. "Marcus is at the back," she said. "With the plants. I'll help you pot them."

We both hurried downstairs and Swan opened the back door for Marcus. He held a plastic storage container in both hands, carried it carefully into the cupboard and placed it on the wide shelf he'd made. "Ta da," he said unexpectedly.

I recognized the smell of pot on both of them and I suspected that they were both high, even though they acted normally. I had never smoked pot—indeed, I had never smoked cigarettes after my first fumbling experiments as a teenager. What would it feel like to be high? I intended to find out some day.

Marcus removed the lid of the container as Swan groped in it and lifted out a seedling about eight inches tall and bright green. "Meet Mary Jane," she said. "Healthy, but unfortunately, like all Marcus's plants, they've got spider mites."

"What are spider mites?" I put on my glasses to peer at the plant.

"Nasty little sucky bugs. Once you've got 'em it's a pain to get rid of 'em."

"Not a good start," I said feeling my elation dwindle.

"We'll dunk them all in Riddit before we plant them," Swan said. "Have you got the pots ready?" She looked into the grow room. "Great."

Marcus fiddled with the gray box. "I'll put one light on so we can see what we're doing." A hum from one ballast announced a glow from the room as the light came on.

There wasn't much room for three people in the cupboard, but Swan squeezed past with a bucket and a bottle she pulled out of her bag. I stood like a bump on a log until she came back to organize us. "Here's a bucket of Riddit. Marcus, you take each plant and dunk them. Then hand them to me and Jess."

"What about the mothers?" Marcus asked.

"Oh yeah. Jess, which plants do you want to be mothers?" Swan looked at me inquiringly.

"What's a mother?"

"They're plants you don't let flower so you can take cuttings from them."

"I've no idea," I said.

"Choose the biggest and the best," Swan said and pulled out a plant. "Like this one. You keep them with the others until you switch. Then they'll have to come in here."

"Switch what?"

"Switch to the flowering cycle when they get twelve hours of darkness. But the mothers still need only six hours of darkness." Swan lifted up a couple of plants before choosing another as a mother.

"Where will I put them? Will I have to remember to take them out of the room every day after six hours?" I was thinking I'd be sure to mess that up.

Swan laughed. "No, Marcus will fix you up with fluorescent lights in here. That's where you'll put your cuttings, too."

"Where are the three-gallons?" Marcus asked.

"By the back door. But I haven't watered them," I said.

"I'll do it," he said and made for the back door.

After a couple of false starts we formed a sort of chain gang. Marcus dunked a plant head first into the bucket, handed it into the grow room, and either Swan or I planted it into one of the prepared pots. It was easy to scrape out a hollow in the damp soil with my hand, gently spread the roots and then pat the soil back.

Before long thirty-two plants reached up to the lights. Marcus planted the two chosen as mothers into the three-gallon pots and made room for them before turning on the remaining three lights. After a few moments he arranged a fan beside each light and turned these on. I understood why we needed so many electrical outlets.

"What are those for?" I said.

"It gets too hot under the lights if you don't have fans on. Particularly in the summer," Swan said. "Keep an eye on the temperature here." She pointed to the new gauge that I'd noticed earlier. "It should be eighty to eighty-five degrees when the lights are on and no less than seventy degrees when they're off. And watch the humidity too, though there's not much you can do about it. Should be fifty to sixty percent."

We stood in a row to admire our handiwork. "Awesome," Swan said.

Marcus moved forward and lowered each light until it was about eighteen inches above the plants. "Raise these as the plants grow," he said looking at me. He wore shorts and a T-shirt, but this time it was his strong arms that attracted me. What a pity he was so inarticulate, because he was quite gorgeous.

"We'll come by tomorrow to make sure everything's okay," Swan said.

"Is there anything I should do?" I said.

"Just make sure everything's working. You'll need to water about every third day," Swan said, "and you feed them every other watering. Have you got food, Marcus?"

"Not yet."

"That's okay. They get food from the soil the first two weeks," Swan said.

"I'll set the lights." Marcus moved to the gray box. "When do you want them off?"

I must have looked blank because Swan said, "They get six hours of darkness. That means the lights are off for six hours and there's no hum. When would you like that to be?"

I thought for a moment. "The evening would be best as that's when I usually have visitors. Say, five to eleven?"

"You want them off when it's hot inside, so that'll be fine."

"It's only ten o'clock now," Marcus said. "I'll set the timer tomorrow."

"Yes, no point in having them off for an hour tonight

when they've only just gone on," Swan said making a move to the stairs.

"I'd like to put saucers under the pots," I said, looking at Marcus. "Is that okay?"

"China ones? Like under tea cups?" His expression was serious.

Was he teasing me? "No, plastic ones. Made for plant pots. So they don't drain on the floor."

"I'll get some." Without another word he went out the back door.

"Seeya," Swan called after him. At the top of the stairs she turned to me and said, "You'll get used to him."

"I am. He's stopped shrugging at everything I say, which is a blessing."

"He likes you," she said. "He thinks you're funny." Then she was off.

I returned to the basement with an old stool that I took into the grow room and sat down. There, before me, lay rows of black pots each containing a small plant with leaves that looked like how a child would draw a leaf: serrated edges and marked indentations running from the center line to the edge—not at all like chrysanthemums.

The room smelled fresh, like a greenhouse, which, I suppose, it was. Oscillating fans swept a breeze over me every few seconds and the little plants fluttered when it was their turn. One little guy was being blown by two fans and didn't have a respite in which to stand up. "Oh you poor luv," I said, and moved one of the fans back a bit and re-positioned him before sitting down again. I should have said 'her' as Swan told me only female marijuana plants flower. Maybe I shouldn't call them 'buddies'? 'My girls' perhaps? Or the 'choir'? No, they all budded so buddies is what I'd call them.

My garden. I surveyed it with pride. I felt like a mother watching her children in a playground: proud, protective, interested in their welfare, willing to nurture them to adulthood.

What would Jason and Amy say? They sometimes dropped in and occasionally came for an early dinner, but that would change when the children were older and went to bed a bit later. They would be upstairs, of course. I don't think Jason had ever seen the basement since we inspected the house prior to purchase. I planned to put a lock on the door to the basement in the hall in case one of the children decided to explore.

It occurred to me that there was nothing to relieve the intense brightness of the room, the heat, the fans; the poor wee plants had no stimuli. I would find them something to look at and some music to listen to.

A short while later I had improved their environment. Three Western Wilderness posters of tall trees, hanging on the white walls, would inspire my buddies to reach for the sky, and an old CD player repeatedly played The Best of Mozart. My cameo brooch, depicting the Goddess of the Harvest, hung from its ribbon on the temperature gauge for further encouragement. I asked Ceres to bless my plants, watch over them and encourage them to grow.

12

THE NEXT MORNING, before I'd even had breakfast, I heard Marcus's truck. I no longer expected him to seek me out or let me know he was there, so I wandered downstairs to find him in the grow room. "What are those?" he asked, pointing to the posters.

"It's very bright in here, sunny and warm, but nothing for the plants to look at," I said. "I thought the tall trees would inspire them."

To my utter astonishment, Marcus laughed. I had never seen him smile before, let alone laugh. "Plants enjoying pictures?" he spluttered.

I didn't know what to say. He made for the back door. "I've set the timer," he said as he left and, "There's saucers." He pointed to a pile of plastic saucers by the door.

I sat on the stool among the plants. What was it with Marcus? One minute he is just a silent presence and the next, he laughs at pictures in the grow room. Would I ever understand him?

Hearing about the laundry room renovation should have been a warning, but it wasn't; Jason's phone call set my heart thumping.

"Hi Mum. You know we're renovating our laundry room, right? We weren't going to get a new washer and dryer, but now we've decided to upgrade to a front-load washer and an energy-efficient dryer. There's nothing wrong with the ones we've got but, you know how it is."

"Yes." I had a horrible premonition of what was coming. It came.

"Would you like our old washer and dryer? There's still plenty of life in them."

"That's very kind of you, luv. I don't have a dryer and my old washer is losing its swish." I tried to sound enthusiastic. How the hell was I going to let him into the basement without him seeing what I was doing?

"Great. Do you have a dryer outlet?"

"Yes, I had a new one put in a while ago when I was saving up for a dryer." Bless Swan for suggesting a second one.

"Good. Well I have a friend here with a truck and he'll help me bring them over."

"What now?" My hand flew to my chest.

"Yes."

I thought quickly. It would take him fifteen minutes to get here. Could I fix things downstairs in that time? "Give me half-an-hour. I'm still in my nightie."

"Fine. Half-an-hour. We'll come round the back."

"I'll open the door for you."

I flew downstairs. My breath came in short pants. My hands trembled so much I could hardly undo the hose from the tap. Get a grip. Take it slowly.

Marcus had put a lock on the cupboard door and the key hung on a nail under the stairs. I unlocked the door and coiled the hose into the cupboard. Then I switched off the lights and turned off the fans. Silence. Now what? The vent tube, of course. I stood on my short stepladder to undo the rope holding the tube up and pulled it out of the chimney. Several yards of concertinaed tube lay at my feet. I tried to gather it up but it acted like an slippery python. "Oh no," I said out loud. "What am I going to do?"

Any minute now there would be a knock at the back door. I wouldn't answer it. I would pretend I was dead. Or having a heart attack. I was close to that anyway.

I blew out hard several times, then folded the tube from one end until I held a manageable pile. I removed the insulation and shoved the whole pile through the hole into the grow room. The insulation was easy to replace. Now push the plastic back. There. Let's hope it will stay there.

I checked around. Nothing untoward to be seen except for the new room, of course. No sound. I sniffed. No smell, but I opened the back door in case.

Just as a truck pulled into the space next to the garage, I noticed that the cupboard door was open. I hastily locked it, pocketed the key and went out to greet Jason and a swarthy young man who made me think of the Mafia.

"Mum, this is Tony. They're bringing the new washer and dryer today so he's helping me get rid...move the old ones."

"Here's where they're going," I said, leading the way into the basement. "You'll have to pull out the old washer first."

"Hey, what's this?" Jason ran a hand down the plastic wall of the grow room. He turned to me with wide eyes.

"Oh, it's a store room I had built," I said casually. "You can make a bit of money renting out a secure storage space."

"Are you going to drywall it?" Jason poked at the plastic.

"Next job," I said. I pointed to the dryer outlet. "That's where the dryer goes."

Jason began to unhook the washer. "Got a wrench?" he asked Tony.

"In the truck. I'll get it."

"I'm sure you'll be happy with a new washer, Mum. And you haven't had a dryer for years, have you?"

"I've never had one here in Nelson. I've always used a washing line. Still will most of the time." I didn't want to sound ungrateful so I added, "But this will be wonderful in the winter and when it's raining. No more damp laundry kicking about." I had lost my indoor lines and the dryer would be a blessing.

Jason soon had the washer unhooked and they both hefted it out. My pulse had stopped racing and I swept the area where the dryer was to go and the floor where the old washer had been.

I sat on the stairs pulling my ear lobe while Jason and Tony carried in the dryer. They had to stop to put it down while Jason moved something out of the way. It was the chimney cover. I had forgotten to put it over the hole when I pulled out the vent tube. I looked up at the exposed hole. Would Jason see any significance in it? Luckily he seemed more interested in attaching the washer and dryer.

I couldn't enjoy Jason's demonstration of how my new appliances worked, nor take in the instructions. Tony must have thought I was batty with my fixed smile and delighted squeaks and nothing sensible to say.

"Anyway, Mum, I remembered to bring the instruction booklets so you can figure it out at your leisure." He took a long look around the basement. "Must go," he said.

"Are you sure you wouldn't like coffee?" I had already asked, but I couldn't think of anything else to say.

"I'll take a rain check." When Jason reached the back door he turned round and gave me a giant hug and lifted me off my feet, like he used to. "Mum, I want you to know I'd never do anything to hurt you."

13

FROM WAKING UP with only a trip to the library or the food bank to look forward to, I now had a garden to tend, two gardens in fact, one indoor and one outdoor. The indoor garden required more attention than I had anticipated. The plants needed water every third day for one thing and the room also required daily inspection to check the temperature and make sure everything was working. I came down one day to find the lights still off and I had to adjust the timer because the little lever hadn't been tightened properly and had slipped. It's a good thing Swan had warned me about this possibility or I would have panicked.

As the plants grew taller, I had to raise the lights. I took a deep breath and placed the stepladder as close as I could to the light. What if I dropped it? It would smash into the plants. I might be electrocuted. I clutched the top bar of my little stepladder and tried to reach out an arm. The lamp, which was turned on, hung by a chain, and because of the shade, I had quite a stretch to reach it. All I had to do was lift and hook the chain on by another link. But if the link wouldn't slide on, or if I let go, I would drop the lot. What if the hook came out? What then? I would be left, like the Statue of Liberty, holding a lamp, possibly forever.

I could wait for Swan or Marcus but I was already too reliant on them and I was not going to act like a little gray mouse. The hook that held the chain was screwed into wood. If I put another hook beside it to hold the last link, it would prevent the light from crashing to the floor should I lose my grip. In no time I had hooks screwed in, the last links secured on them and I could move the chain without worry.

Although walking around watering was easy, assessing how much water to deliver was not. Swan had told me to water until it seeped out of the bottom of the pots but eventually I learned to count for the length of time I judged to be enough: one and two and three, up to nine, next plant, one and two and three. It was hypnotic standing in the heat of the lamps, counting like a mantra, but I had to concentrate or I would miss one.

The first time this happened, I discovered a wilting plant two days after watering. The poor little thing. I apologized to her, stroked her leaves, and gave her a good dousing. The next day she was fine—marijuana is a weed after all. After that, my watering routine ended with a careful check that no one had been missed.

I also had to look out for my own welfare. Like most women of my age, I had a fear of falling and not being found for days. As a precaution I took a phone with me when I went downstairs, but rather than carry it on me I made the mistake of just leaving it handy. So when I tripped over the hose and fell, I was helpless.

Bloody hell, I've gone and done it now. I lay in a heap between the pots, my head cushioned in a plant, staring up into a 1000-watt light bulb. I tested my legs; they seemed to move all right. It was my arms that didn't respond. *Bugger.* My shirt had caught in the pallet that supported me and the pots. The more I struggled the tighter it pulled around my throat.

I made myself take deep breaths and relax. After a few moments, I managed to release one arm from its stranglehold and undo the buttons of my shirt. That took the pressure off my neck. The next task was to stand up. I tried to do this without damaging any more buddies, but I had to squash another one when I rolled over. Once on my front I was able to get onto my knees and inspect the plants before me at eye level.

At my age I always took advantage of being on the ground, since it is such a job to stand up again, so I inspected the underside of the leaves for signs of nutritional defects. I fluffed out the plant that had been a pillow and tried to restore the one I had crushed, but it had lost a whole branch. I stood up and stroked the remaining branches with soothing murmurs of repentance and wishes for a quick recovery, but she looked a sorry sight. I went upstairs for Rescue Remedy, a homeopathic emergency medicine, and shook a few drops on her leaves.

For myself? I made a cup of tea.

The time came to feed the plants. Marcus had provided two jugs, one of SuperCropA and one of SuperCropB/Grow, each with instructions about the amount to use. The garbage can reservoir held about 130 litres. Of course the liquid food was calculated in quarts so, after much ado with a calculator and a pencil, I figured a cup of each in the reservoir would be right.

The spider mites had risen again. At some point Marcus had brought in a sprayer and a bottle of neem oil with instructions to spray every few days and to wear a mask. Damn Marcus. Surely he could have set me up with healthy plants? Instead, he'd brought me infested cuttings leaving me with a chronic problem that neem oil did little to cure.

As Swan had said, Marcus was a whiz with electricity and building, but when it came to plant care he didn't have a clue—neither did Swan when it came down to it. Both of them had mentioned regular pruning, but had not said how, so I simply snipped away with scissors until there was more greenery on the floor than on the plants. I gathered it all up to stuff into a garbage bag. By this time the plants were beginning to smell, a sweetish smell that was quite distinctive. What was I to do with the garbage? I couldn't put it out with the regular garbage—that would be a real give-away. It would have to wait until the end when we'd have to get rid of all the plants. But it had to be stored somewhere and the basement was becoming quite crowded. I stashed the bag near the back door. If unexpected visitors arrived, I'd have to deal with the problem then.

I needed advice, but where would I find it? The Internet at the library was a good source, but I didn't like to write "marijuana growing" in the Search box in case someone looked over my shoulder. There didn't seem to be any books on the subject either. Not only that, Marcus and Swan, who had been around almost daily, had now evaporated. Was it deliberate? To show me that it was my garden, that they were only there to start me up, that I was to do all the work? That would be fine—if I knew what to do.

Then Marcus appeared at the front door. He usually came through the back door into the basement with a task in mind, so a knock at the front meant he needed to talk to me.

"I'm going away," he said without preamble. "Tree planting."

"How nice," I said.

"Here's some money." He handed me a $100 bill. "For SuperCropB/Bloom. And Mighty Bud."

"Oh yes. When do I use those?"

"When you switch."

"Where do I get them?"

"The shop near the airstrip."

"Right." *Switch* meant turn the lights to a twelve-hour cycle so the plants would flower, but what was the food? Maybe the shop would tell me.

This exchange had taken place with Marcus holding onto the knob on the inside of the front door, as if ready to make a run for it. He suddenly swung the door open, uncoiled his tense body and almost leapt into the garden.

"Marcus," I said firmly. "Wait."

He stopped and looked at me like a dog obeying the 'sit' command. "Don't you want to look at the plants?"

"Why? What's wrong?"

"Nothing. Except spider mites. But I thought you might be interested. And I would like to know if they're ready to switch."

"Oh. Okay."

I unlocked the inside door to the basement and followed him down. He poked his head into the grow room, stared, and entered with what seemed like caution.

"What's wrong?" I asked.

"You been pruning?"

"Yes. But I don't know how. Why?"

"Small buds."

I wanted to shake him. "If you show me what to do, I'll do it. But I need instruction."

He didn't say anything but started to go upstairs.

"Are they ready to switch?"

"Yes."

The conversation, if you could call it that, was clearly over. I would put a call in for Swan.

"When are you back?" I called after his retreating figure.

"September."

I was still clutching the $100 bill. They had occasionally shown up at the Grill but I'd never owned one before. I fingered it gingerly and held it up to the light. What if it was a forgery? How would I explain how I came by it?

"I got it from the bank, Your Honor. When I drew money out."

"You have nothing in your account, Mrs. Kemp. Where did this note come from?"

"I don't know, Your Honor."

"You don't know? Take her down."

This sort of scene playing in my head didn't help me approach the grow shop. It looked like a regular gardening store, but I half expected to see plainclothes police spying on it from the bushes. I parked several yards away, sauntered past, stared in the window and, when no one was in sight, slipped in.

Neatly stacked shelves held jugs of plant food, large light bulbs wrapped in corrugated cardboard, smaller containers of things like hydrogen peroxide and calcium, bags of worm droppings, bat guano, everything healthy or ailing plants might need.

Before I had time to examine the outer shelves laden with timers and gadgets, a tall, clean-shaven young man, wearing those silky shorts with a stripe around the hem, appeared from a door at the back. "Good morning," he said pleasantly. "Can I help you?"

"I'm looking for SuperCropB/Bloom," I said, "and Mighty Bud."

He didn't seem at all surprised, but walked past me to reach for a gallon jug and a smaller bottle that he took over to the counter. It was all so natural—like purchasing shampoo.

"Anything else?" he asked.

"No thank you."

"That will be $66.20."

I handed over the $100 note that he took without comment and gave me change.

"Would you like a bag?"

"Oh, yes please. I forgot my shopping bag." He put the two bottles into a black plastic bag and laid it on the counter. He didn't seem to be in any hurry; in fact he leaned on the counter as if ready to share confidences. Beside him, on the counter, a printed notice advised shoppers that talking about illegal substances was forbidden.

There were no other customers so I asked in a low voice, "Can you tell me about pruning?"

The young man bent closer. "Pardon," he said.

I looked around again and repeated my question.

"Sure," he said in normal tones. "What stage are your plants at?"

"They're about this tall." I spread my hands about two feet apart. "But I don't know how to prune and I haven't done them properly. Just snipped away randomly."

He took a piece of paper and a pen and drew a plant. "Those are leaves. You don't cut those. The plant needs them. These are the shoots that are going to flower. Those are the ones you have to control. At first pruning you cut those down to four per plant. That way you end up with four big buds and not lots of little ones."

"I'm too late for that," I said.

"Yes, but you can still get some control. Choose about six to develop and then snip off all the others. Then the energy will go into the ones that you've left." He leaned on the counter again. "If your plants are that tall you must be ready to put them into flower?"

"I guess so." Marcus had gone off leaving no specific directions so I decided to go ahead and do it anyway. "What's your name?" I asked wondering what the protocol about introductions was.

"Michael," he said. "And that's Pilot." Michael indicated a short, older man with cropped gray hair and one earing who was unloading boxes. "Feel free to ask either of us questions any time."

I wanted to pour out my worries about how I didn't know what I was doing, but I just said, "I've got spider mites. I inherited them."

"What are you doing about them?"

"Spraying with neem oil."

"That's all you can do right now, but after flowering, turn the fans off, leave the lights on for three days, then let off a Doctor Doom. That should be the end of them." Michael produced a canister. I assumed it contained pesticide.

"I'll get one later." Then I thought I'd better get one while I had the money and Michael added it to my bag.

I was sure Marcus wouldn't ask about the money or expect any change; anyway it was only a loan that I would pay back eventually, so why shouldn't I spend it?

"How much food are you giving?" Michael asked.

"I give what they say on the label. Add it to the water."

"What do you know about PPM?"

I stared at him. "Post-partum um, er, mood?"

Michael laughed. "Parts per million. An accurate way of figuring out how much food your plants need is to measure the PPM of the run off and estimate the PPM of the mix."

"How do I do that?"

"With a PPM meter." Michael stretched an arm over to where assorted gizmos hung and handed me a long glass rod, much like a thermometer. "You just stick this in the water and read it."

"What should it say?"

Michael explained what different measures of PPM

meant and how to adjust the food accordingly. "Here, I'll print it out for you." He turned to his computer and before long I heard the printer hum. He returned and handed me a sheet of paper with the PPM levels needed by, for example, Flowering stage: 1000-1400.

"How much is this?" I held up the meter.

"Thirty-five dollars."

I looked at my change. It came to about twenty dollars. "This is the only money I have. I'll get it next time."

"You have enough there," Michael said. He handed me a new meter in a box. "Come in any time if you have questions."

I left as a pro. I now knew how to prune and I could hardly wait to get to my garden and begin. And I knew how to get rid of the damn spider mites. And not only that, I knew how to feed accurately.

I was grateful to Marcus and Swan, but why didn't they know all I'd learned in an hour in the grow shop? Perhaps Marcus didn't have a garden? Swan had said his plants always had spider mites so I had assumed he must have grown them. He had never said he did. He could have got the infested seedlings from someone else who always had spider mites. Swan didn't grow—she lived in an apartment.

Pruning seemed such an important part of the whole business yet neither of them knew how to do it; at least, they had never shown me. Well from then on, I was going to be in charge. I was going to make the decisions. I was the Mistress of my garden.

The next morning I was up early and set to prune. The bed-side table from the spare room became a pot holder so that the plant was at a height where I could see what I was doing. It seemed silly to cut off potential buds, but Michael had stressed the futility of growing tiny buds. I reckoned that a plant had only so much oomph and that should be used by the few rather than the many. Although he said not to remove leaves during the grow stage, he had also said to take off the bottom leaves of the plant before flowering.

After a while, I got the idea and snipped away with confidence. I must say the plants looked better for my efforts—as if they had had manicures. I gave each a careful spray of neem oil before putting them back under their lights. Another bag of clippings joined the other.

Using my new PPM meter as a guide, I added food to the water and watered the garden. It was time to switch to a twelve-hour light cycle. Noon to midnight was good for the lights to be off as it still gave me time in the morning to work. Swan had told me how important it was to not put any light on during the dark time as the plants revert back to a vegetative state very readily, so I could not work when the lights were off.

When I went back upstairs the strong smell of growing garden hit me. I sniffed around. It was me that stank—my shirt, hands, arms, and probably hair. A quick change and a wash and I could present myself at the door if need be, but I set aside a shirt and a long apron to wear downstairs and hung it inside the door to the basement.

As I chomped on a grilled cheese sandwich, I suddenly remembered I'd left the mothers in the grow room. They still needed only six hours of darkness or they too would flower and then couldn't be used for cuttings. I rushed downstairs to move them into the cupboard and under the stack of fluorescent lights Marcus had set up.

The mothers, in their larger pots, were now bushy and bigger than the rest and not pruned because the flower sites would become cuttings to grow into seedlings for the next crop. I wasn't sure when to take cuttings, or how, but now I had found an advisor, I would visit him for a lesson.

I had more or less given up on Swan; I'd seen neither hide nor hair of her for at least two weeks and there had been no response to my calls. Maybe she was away too? When she showed up that evening she looked dreadful—dank dark hair with no dye, smeared mascara, blotchy face. She had obviously been crying.

"Oh you poor wee thing," I said. "Whatever is the matter?" I put my arms around her and she snuggled into me and cried into my shoulder.

When the first flood had abated I led her into the kitchen, sat her down, and put the kettle on. "I'll make us some tea. Now, tell me all about it."

"I lost my job. Business is down. And Milo is shacked up with some skank." She looked at me sheepishly. "Sorry." The floodgates opened again and I reached for a box of tissues.

I could barely make out what she was saying, but the gist of it was that the boyfriend she had been living with had been two-timing her while she was at work.

"I came home when I was fired and found them in our bed. *Our* bed. In *my* apartment. Bastard. Cheating asshole." She thumped on the table calling Milo names I had never thought of using, but I understood the emotion well enough.

Before I met Frank I'd dated Trevor, a handsome local hero with a Triumph. To own a car in my young day, where I grew up, was quite something and I was thrilled when he asked me out for a spin in the Dales. I was too innocent to understand that I was to reward him for his favors in an unused barn.

I can see and smell that barn to this day. Stone walls with draughty apertures, packed soil and cow dung floor, wooden feeding trough along one wall. Trevor laid a blanket down and began my education into the adult world.

I fell in love. At least, I thought it was love. Everywhere I went I looked for him; no matter what I was doing he was in my thoughts; my dreams were of him in evening suit and me in a long, chiffon dress dancing down a wide sweeping marble staircase.

Then one day, as I walked down the High Street, a Triumph roared past, top down, Mabel Higginbottom in the passenger seat. Mabel Higginbottom with her Toni perm and her false eyelashes. She had the gall to wave to me. I wanted to throttle her—slowly—with a garrotte.

And as for Trevor…. Well, I knew exactly how poor little Swan was feeling. I just listened to her, made 'there, there' noises and filled her teacup. Eventually her sorrow changed to energizing anger. "When I get home I'm going to throw all his stuff out the window. After I've ripped the shit out of his tighty-whiteys. Bastard."

"That'll teach him," I said.

Swan blew her nose. "How are you, Jess? How's the garden? Must be time to switch."

"Yes, I just did."

"So that means," she took the calendar off the wall, found the day's date, counted eight weeks, "harvest time will be middle of September, say the eighteenth. I can come and trim. I'll see if Marcus will be back, but if he isn't I'll find someone else."

"What do I need to do?"

"There should be room near the door for everyone to sit. They need a good light. I'll explain closer to the date." Swan stood up as if ready to leave.

"I went to the grow shop a couple of days ago. Met Michael."

"Yeah. He knows a lot."

"He told me how to prune. I hadn't been doing it properly."

"I don't know how to prune. I really only help with trimming and I water for people when they're away, but I don't know much about plants. You'll have to show me."

"Neither does Marcus." I stood up to put the cups on the draining board.

"No, he grows outdoors mostly."

Ahh, so that was it. Outdoor growing was a whole different ball game. If they didn't prune the plants the same as indoor ones that would explain why Marcus didn't know how and why he knew nothing about indoor pests like spider mites. *Tree planting indeed.*

I turned to Swan. "The next thing I have to find out about is how to take cuttings. I guess it's time?"

"I've done that a couple of times. You need a bunch of jiffy pots and a couple of trays with domes. I'll get them for you, if you want. And I'll bring you a book."

Swan left with promises to come back with the book and to help me take cuttings.

14

THE PLAN FOR the next Crones' meeting was to discuss books we were reading. Swan had got me *Indoor Marijuana Horticulture,* but it didn't lend itself to discussion in that company. I arrived with a copy of *How Green was my Valley* instead.

There were twelve of us, each armed with a book and ready to sit in a circle. Ed dropped Eva off as usual and Maggie helped her in while Joan fussed over Nina.

Some Crones attended meetings regularly, whereas others were sporadic. The latter group included Thelma, an eighty-four-year old former ballet dancer. I smiled when she arrived. Thelma was always good for a laugh. She once had us all lie on the floor to see how far we could lift a leg and extend it over our heads. Most of us thought we were doing well to lift a leg at all, but Thelma could practically touch the floor behind her head. It was her smirk as she reviewed our prostrate, panting forms that made me chuckle.

We started every meeting with a check-in on how people

are doing. Sometimes this activity took most of our time, as it did on that occasion.

Joan reported on Laura. "She's at home being cared for by a niece, but she keeps going to the hospital wanting more tests."

"Have they found out what's wrong with her?"

"No. Something neurological they say, but they don't know what."

"Has anyone been to see her?"

"I went when she was in the hospital," I said. "She wasn't so good; couldn't walk or even stand for long."

"If she got herself off those damned drugs she'd be a lot better," Maggie said. "Especially the statins. She's showing typical side effects. But she won't listen. Speaking of drugs…" Maggie got up to hand everyone a cup of coffee.

The church basement was quite bright in the summer as the sunlight streamed in a row of windows and gave the indoor-outdoor carpet the appearance of grass. I wanted to get out a deckchair. It was certainly warm enough as the church always cranked up the heat for our meeting, even in the summer.

"I'll do some baking and take it to her," Jane said when we were all settled with a cup.

"She won't eat."

"What? Not even when the doctor tells her to?" Jane rolled her eyes. "I'll try anyway."

When it was my turn to report I said, "I've followed up on a couple of jobs. One was quite promising—looking after an elderly gentleman while his daughter is at work, but they only wanted to pay five dollars an hour."

"What?" Maggie said. "That's disgusting. How are you expected to live on that?"

"There are always people who want something for nothing," Jane said.

Claire chimed in with, "That's patriarchy for you."

She never mentioned she'd seen me at the food bank, bless her, so she could mention patriarchy as much as she wanted.

"They either don't want to pay or they want someone younger," I said.

One value of the Crones was to be honest with each other and keep what people said confidential. I really wanted to say, "I'm a bit worried about my plants; their leaves are yellow at the edges. Maybe I'm using the wrong food and they're not getting enough nitrogen." They would probably become dumb with shock if they knew what I was doing and anyway, one value of growers is never to talk about it.

Eva busied herself by opening and closing a black, plastic purse that had a stiff metal clasp. Her trembling fingers groped at the clasp until it finally opened with an irritating click. Then she foraged in the depths, producing a sound of rustling paper before closing the bag again with another click. We enjoyed a few seconds of silence from her while she hugged the bag to her chest as she looked around triumphantly. Then she started the whole performance again.

Someone asked her how she was. She looked around as though she didn't know us, smiled her fatuous smile and said, "Give and thou shalt receive."

Thelma spoke next. She must have been a stunner in her youth with her round, baby-blue eyes, her sensuous mouth, and her lithe body. Age had treated her well; few wrinkles and a general porcelain doll-like appearance that matched her little-girl voice with its slight lisp. As we hadn't seen her for a while, we leaned forward to hear her news. To my surprise the baby-blues filled with tears and she couldn't speak.

We waited until she finally blurted out, "George wants a divorce."

"What?"

Eva broke the shocked silence with a click and a rustle. Maggie moved to stand behind Thelma so she could massage her shoulders. "Take your time," Maggie said.

Thelma groped in her pocket for a tissue. "We've been married sixty years. We had our sixtieth in February. Now he wants a divorce. All because…all because…" She buried her face in her hands.

We waited expectantly. Maggie continued to massage.

Finally Thelma was able to say, "I had an affair. It only lasted three months; with the theater electrician. A beautiful example of the male form." She stopped crying and smiled as if she could see him before her. "George was away on a course at the time. I broke it off when he came home."

"How long ago was this?" I asked.

"Let me see. It was before I had the kids. I had been married three, no, four years, so it would be fifty-six years ago."

"And he wants a divorce *now*?"

"How did he find out?" Jane asked.

"I kept Patrick's love letters. I like to read them once in a while. When I feel low. He made me feel so, so…beautiful." Tears flowed again.

"How did George find them?"

"That's what I don't understand. They were under my panties."

"Why would George go poking around in your underwear?" I asked.

Maggie returned to her seat. "So you've been married sixty years and George discovers you had an affair fifty-six years ago and wants a divorce?" Maggie sounded as incredulous as the rest of us. "How old is he?"

"Ninety-four," Thelma answered.

I wanted to crack up and struggled to control myself by holding my belly tight and clenching my teeth. Then I caught Jane's eye and she smiled. I looked away, but started to shake. Then someone snorted and that did it. Everyone broke into uncontrollable laughter. Thelma looked hurt for a minute, and slowly smiled. Finally she was laughing like the rest of us. People rocked in their chairs, someone got up and rushed to the toilet, and we all enjoyed that mirth that leaves you aching and looking at your friends with affection.

Everyone reached for a tissue and Thelma wiped her eyes again, but this time for tears of laughter. "He said I had deceived him and he's going to woo Chloe, a woman his age in our complex. So he's bought himself a straw Panama hat for the summer."

We all howled again. The thought of George, a feeble old man if ever there was one, in a straw Panama, bowing over the hand of an equally aged woman, made my day.

"I feel better for that," Thelma said. "Silly old fool. Let him rot in hell."

"Are you still living with him?"

Thelma and George lived in a retirement complex that provided housekeeping and a main meal.

"I had to for a couple of weeks. We were in a two-bed-room apartment, but they've found me a one-bedroom and a bachelor for him. So now we're fighting over the furniture."

"Don't you have meals together?"

"Just dinner. But I don't sit with him. Chloe does." Thelma fluttered her eyelashes and simpered, "Oh George, dear, would you like me to cut up your meat?" She got up and sashayed across the room casting each of us a 'come hither' look before sitting down again. "I had to get the staff to guard our apartment while we moved. He and a couple of other old codgers carried away my recliner chair while I was out. I caught them in the hall, so I sat in it and screamed."

I'd tried to practice a scream once—in the car. It's very difficult to do, but Thelma, of course, had been on the stage.

"What happened?"

"The staff came and moved it back. Told George nothing is to be touched until the legal stuff is finished. They took his key." She raised both arms in a V.

Eva stood up, which is usually the sign that she wants the bathroom. Maggie took her, leaving the purse on the chair. Before long a cry like a distressed cat emitted from the toilet and Eva, peeing down her leg, ran out.

"Shoot, I should have taken the purse with her." Maggie grabbed it, but as it was open, the contents spilled on to the floor. Maggie scooped up most of the items, thrust the purse at Eva and helped her back into the toilet. I picked up an envelope and a black and white studio photo fell out. It showed a glamorous woman with wavy black hair, a wide, cheerful smile, and calm, tender eyes. She could have been a film star but no, it was a young Eva. I stared at the picture. I felt a lump in my throat as tears came into my eyes.

How much longer could we handle Eva? Or, more importantly, how much longer could Ed handle her dementia? He did not want her to go into a home, but he was no spring chicken himself. His respite of two hours while she was with us was about his only time off. When I first met Eva she was a lively, active woman who fostered handicapped children and who enjoyed the outdoor activities she organized for them. Ed must love her dearly to continue to care for her in such a state.

When Ed came for Eva I helped her into the car trying to ignore her wet dress and making sure her purse was in her hands. As I waved them off it was the cheerful face and the serene smile of the real Eva who looked out of the window. What a supreme irony: Eva, who for years looked after the mentally handicapped, now needed such care herself.

Couples: Ed and Eva, Thelma and George, Frank and me. What would my life be like if I'd stayed with Frank? I certainly wouldn't be poor. Frank had his own plumbing business and was never short of work. We were together about fifteen years, until the children were teenagers. What went wrong? We had both grown up knowing what our roles were: his to clean gutters, do repairs, mow the lawn; mine to cook, clean, look after the children. My view shattered after reading Germaine Greer's *The Female Eunuch* and poor Frank, who had no equivalent male wake-up call, had to deal with a furious wife who was no longer content to do all the housework.

Divorce was the only way we knew how to handle this state of affairs.

The Crones never did discuss books that day, but what the hell? Life is stranger than fiction.

15

I VISITED the grow shop again and asked Michael about taking cuttings. He printed out a sheet of directions for me. In addition to the jiffy pots and trays that Swan was getting, I needed Vitamin B and rooting gel. I was able to buy them as they didn't cost much, so when Swan arrived to help me, everything was ready.

We set to work in the cupboard. Since the lights in the grow room were off, it was quite cool in there even with the fluorescents on. A small bucket of tepid water held sixty jiffy pots soaking until they expanded and a large bowl of warm water with Vitamin B in it was ready to receive the cuttings. I had searched through my embroidery stuff and found really sharp scissors and with rooting gel in a ramekin we were ready.

Swan looked more like her usual self with a piece of orange hair running down the back of her head. She'd got over the treacherous Milo and as we squeezed the jiffy pots until they weren't dripping, she told me all about her new boyfriend. "He just moved to Nelson. He's a mechanic."

"That can be useful. Look, open the slit of each jiffy wide enough to put the stalk in."

"I can do that." Swan began to fill two trays with wet jiffies. "He's got a regular job too. He's the first boyfriend I've ever had with regular hours."

I turned to the mother plants and inspected one for suitable shoots. "What's his name?"

"Sam."

I looked at her in mock surprise. "Sam? You mean you have a boyfriend with an ordinary name?"

She laughed. "There. The jiffies are ready. Now what?"

"We start cutting shoots. The key is to not let an air bubble get into the stalk, so you have to make a clean cut and quickly put the cutting into water." I pulled at a branch, selected a shoot, cut it and transferred it to the bowl of water.

Swan picked up the printout from Michael. "The shoots should have three leaves," she said. "You know, Sam is the first boyfriend I've had who doesn't grow and doesn't smoke. He's a health freak."

"In what way?"

"He works out every day with weights and won't eat chips."

"Sounds good."

When ten shoots rested in the water I lined up the gel pot next to the jiffies and said, "Right. Here we go. You cut off the end again under water, dip it into the gel for a few moments…and then into a jiffy. Squeeze the top of the jiffy to hold the stalk, like this, and Bob's your uncle. I think that's right."

Swan said, "You do the cutting and I'll squeeze the jiffies and arrange them on the tray." She began to work and then said, "He's respectful. I like that. And he's clean. Doesn't leave his underwear on the floor, or his smelly socks."

"What do you look for in a guy?" I cut more shoots.

Swan stopped compressing jiffy pots and thought for a moment. "After Milo, loyalty I guess. Personal hygiene. Sweat is not sexy. Someone who wants a girlfriend, not a mother." She carried on preparing the pots. "Intelligent of course. Can hold a conversation and that means listening, not just talking. How many's that?"

"Forty. Only twenty to go."

"A sense of humor is good. Sam doesn't have one unfortunately. He has a lawyer buddy, Luke. Luke went out with Nance a couple of times. As soon as things started looking serious he gave her a contract to sign."

I laughed. "Good grief."

"Yeah. I nearly died laughing. But Sam was dead serious. He thought Luke was great. I told him not to even think of trying the same thing with me."

We soon had thirty cuttings in each tray and Swan lovingly placed a see-through dome over them and then lowered the stack of fluorescent lights until they were close to the top of the domes. "I think you leave the lights on all the time don't you?" she asked.

"Oh, I didn't ask about that. I'll see what the book says. I know I have to mist them twice a day with Vitamin B solution and wipe down the domes." I looked at the remains of the mother plants drooping over their pots. "Thank you Mums. You produced some wonderful offspring."

Swan took a construction garbage bag out of a box and emptied the mothers and their soil into it. "Where do you want this?"

"There's a stack by the back door. I don't know what I'm going to do with them."

"Wait until harvest when you have to empty all the pots. Then you take them to the dump."

"Don't they smell?"

"Yes, but it doesn't matter. You throw them into the containers yourself. I'll help you."

"I've never been to the dump. There's always been someone else to take stuff."

"You drive on. They weigh you. You drive to the Household bin, throw the bags into it, drive back on to the scale, pay, and that's it. Easy peasy."

"Don't I need a truck?"

"Nah. Your car should be big enough. Gotta go." Swan gave me a big hug and left in her usual whirl, a whirl that disturbed the atmosphere. What influence would Sam have on her? If he tried to control her and squash her spirit he'd be ready to join the Vienna Boys' Choir if I had anything to do with it.

There was something endearing about Swan—a sort of innocence. She was the type of person who attracted dogs and small children who wouldn't care what she looked like. Swan would never give away my secret. As a member of the growing community, she followed the unwritten rule to never discuss growing in public or on the phone.

Jason and family were away on holiday. I would ask them for dinner when they got back. I hadn't had them over for ages, largely because of lack of room, but the weather was good enough to use the deck. Should I include Swan? Amy would likely croak when she saw the type of person I hung out with, but the kids would love her. Yes, I would ask her and watch Amy's reaction.

16

"HI MUM, I've got a present for you. Guess what?" Jason's voice sounded cheerful on the phone.

"A crab? Oysters?"

"No. A computer! One of my clients upgraded recently and sold off his laptops really cheap so I got you one."

"That's very good of you, luv, but…"

"I know you've been using the computer at the library and I also know you don't want to turn into an old fuddy-duddy, so I think you'll enjoy it. I'll set it up so you'll have an email account and Internet access. Then you can email Lisa."

I had balked when he first suggested a computer, but since then the idea had grown tempting, especially since it would mean being more in touch with Lisa. And, I had to admit, using the Internet at the library and being able to look up so many things had become a habit. If I got stuck I could always call on Jason, though Amy had made a fuss about him helping me when he'd first suggested it. Maybe we wouldn't tell her.

Jason told me about the cottage they'd rented right on the beach and how Nicholas had enjoyed the fishing net I'd given him and how they'd watched an eagle fishing every morning. "I'll give you the computer when you come on Sunday," Jason continued.

"Actually, I was going to ask you all for dinner," I said. "It's ages since you were all over and we can sit on the deck where there's more room. Can you come on Wednesday?"

"I'll check with Amy. That will be great, but are you sure you want us in the house?"

"Of course. Why not?"

"Right. I'll bring the laptop then and help you set it up. I also have a printer."

"Oh, I don't think I'll be printing anything." I didn't have an office or a suitable space.

"You never know," Jason said.

Wednesday arrived with the blessing of pork chops at the food bank. I had hoarded a previous supply of sausages and hamburgers in the freezer, so I had enough meat to give people choices. Swan could come and promised to arrive early to help me. She also said she would bring a salad, so with an apple pie I'd made, I was all set.

Ingredients for baking were readily obtainable from the food bank. They didn't seem to be in heavy demand, perhaps because people didn't bake from scratch anymore. But I still made my own pastry and cakes, although not bread as it's a lot of effort for one person.

I marinated the chops, lit my little charcoal barbecue in good time, and got spuds ready to make the fries the kids love. It was hot in the sun, but my deck faced north and was nice and cool.

One major preparation was to check my basket of toys. As the children hadn't been to my place for months, it had sat unused, but much of it was still functional: stickers, a floor puzzle, lace cards, trucks, and a tea set.

Swan arrived carrying a colorful bag over one shoulder and holding a large wooden bowl that held a fresh-looking salad with seeds sprinkled on it. She hung the bag on a kitchen chair and said, "Stuff for the kids."

I had been hoping she would appear her most bizarre and she didn't disappoint me. Her hair, slightly longer now, looked as if she'd had an electric shock. It stood straight up in the air, held there by some sort of glossy glue. Some of the sprouts were pink with sparkly things in them so that her head looked like an ornamental cabbage.

Two pieces of metal were implanted in her face: a ring in her upper lip and a stud in the furrow between her nose and lip. Just seeing them brought tears to my eyes—imagine the pain of putting them in. Her eyes were huge with dilated pupils, as if she'd just had them examined by an optician, and gave her a startled look like an animal caught in headlights. How had she achieved that effect? Was it drugs? She seemed clear-headed enough.

A sleeveless top revealed a dragon, with a rose in its mouth, tattooed on one shoulder. I pointed to it. "Is that new? What does it mean?"

She peered at her shoulder as if she had never seen it before. "I was born under the dragon. Chinese. The rose means love."

"Oh, I see."

A very short and tight black skirt hung below the tank top and covered red and yellow striped tights that she surely must have obtained from a sale of Shakespearean costumes at the theater.

Straight-laced Amy would not approve of her. I smiled.

I suppose I should have felt guilty about wanting to get a rise out of Amy but I didn't. She reminded me of my Great Aunt Harriet who always looked as if she had a bad smell under her nose and who had looked down on us kids as if we had head lice. Quite often we did, but not after vinegar treatment, and anyway, she never ever had another expression on her face. So, of course, we wanted to play tricks on her. My brother once sealed her handbag shut with chewing gum but he got such a walloping we never dared try another.

"How's Sam working out?"

She turned to me with a huge smile and bright eyes. "I think I'm in love. He's the best man I've ever had. Thoughtful. Tender. Picks up after himself. Helps around the house."

"Sounds like his mother did a good job."

The front door opened and Jason backed in carrying two cardboard boxes. "Hi, Mum, where should I put these?"

Before I could answer, Nicholas pushed past him to give me a hug, closely followed by Amy holding Julie's hand. Amy wore neat, pressed white shorts and a lime green fitted shirt, tucked into her belt. As always, her hair was immaculate, her nails manicured, and she smelled of expensive perfume.

Everyone bunched in the hall until I said, "In the living room for now, Jason. Hello Amy, come on in."

In the kitchen I introduced Swan as my former co-worker

to Amy and the children. If Amy was aghast at Swan's appearance, she didn't show it. The children, however, were mesmerized. When Swan said, "Kids, check this out," they followed her to the table and began to work on the puzzle books she had brought. She sat with them, pointed out where to start a maze to Nicholas and helped Julie place stickers on outlined figures.

Amy barely said hello when she arrived, but went straight out and sat on the balcony with her back to the kitchen.

Jason came out and said to her, "Have you got that box I gave you to bring in?"

Amy continued to stare at the mountain. "No."

"Is it in the car?" Jason sounded impatient.

"How should I know?" Amy got up, pushed past Jason to move into the kitchen. She poured herself a glass of wine.

Jason glared at her, but didn't say anything. He moved back into the living room and called out, "Come and see this, Mum."

Swan turned to me and said, "Why don't you go look at your new laptop? Amy and I'll watch the barbecue, won't we Amy?"

"Sure," Amy said.

"Right, I'll put the fries in the oven and then I'll have thirty minutes."

Jason had the laptop open on the living room sofa. "The nice thing about a laptop, Mum, is that you're not tied to one place. Once the battery is charged you've got about two hours to move it anywhere."

"What about the printer?" I said. "That has to be in one place, surely?"

"Yes. I tell you what; I'll drop by some other time and set that up for you. Right now I want to show you how this works."

His enthusiasm was infectious and by the end of his demonstration I could hardly wait to play with my new toy. I returned to the kitchen to find the children absorbed with cutouts and Amy and Swan on the balcony sipping wine and engrossed in conversation as they tended the barbecue.

"They're good for tourism," Swan was saying as she flipped a hamburger.

"Maybe," Amy said. "But they're all into drugs."

"Have you ever been out there? There's tight security."

"No, I haven't. The tickets are four hundred dollars! Four hundred dollars to have your eardrums blasted! I already have two kids to keep me awake at night. I don't need blaring music."

Swan laughed. "It's turned into a world class music festival. People save up to come to Shambala. You should try it."

"I don't think I have the right wardrobe. I knew it was time for Shambala when I saw a guy with bright yellow pants, no shirt, and a mock leopard skin jacket walking down Baker Street."

"I saw him too," I joined in. "He looked like a cross between Tarzan and Bozo the clown."

Amy set places at the table for the children.

"I think it's awesome. It started with the kids on the farm wanting to host a dance party for their friends, you know, and it grew and grew. Now ten thousand people come from all over the world. Tickets sell out months before." Swan energetically poked a sausage. "You should be grateful for how much money they bring into the community."

"Well, you have a point. All the shops sell out of camping gear and the grocery shelves are bare," Amy said. "But it's the people hanging out all over Baker Street afterward that bothers me. They block the sidewalk, have their dogs running loose, and play drums all day. It's a good thing there's a by-law now."

"Nelson by-laws are lame. Seriously, no dogs on Baker Street? What kind of town does that? And no hacky-sacking? It's like we're in a dictatorship."

"They also smoke marijuana right on the sidewalk. I don't want my kids exposed to that. First it's pot and then it leads to hard drugs like cocaine." Amy had her official social worker voice on again.

"Nah," Swan said. "That's what *they* want you to believe. It's just not true." She turned to me. "I think everything's cooked now."

I was gobsmacked. I was quite sure that Amy would have found Swan impossible to deal with, but there they were acting like the best of friends and talking calmly about a topic they each had very different views about. Not only that, Nicholas who usually paid me a lot of attention, was now cuddling up to Swan as if I didn't exist.

Jason came out on the deck and he and Amy carefully ignored each other. What was their row about? That's married life for you.

Everything tastes better outdoors, especially meat that has been cooked on charcoal. I could tell Julie, normally a picky eater, enjoyed the food—she let out a continuous *yum-yum* sound.

Nicholas spilled his juice and it was Swan who jumped up to get a cloth and sponge him down. "That silly juice," she said gently. "Juice, you stay in that cup now and be more careful, okay?"

Amy, who had made a move to deal with the spill, sat back with a smile and took a large gulp of wine. She and Jason continued to look anywhere but at each other.

"You're really good with kids," I said to Swan as we stacked dishes.

"I've got a gazillion cousins," she said. "I'll do these dishes later. I promised Nicholas I'd show him cat's cradle."

Amy wandered in as I made tea and refilled her wine glass. "The house looks good," she said. "I can see why you don't want to leave it. I was looking over the balcony at your garden. I didn't know you had a green thumb."

"I don't," I answered. "It's just that I've had time to garden now that I'm not working. I've wanted to grow my own vegetables for years."

"Can I go down and take a closer look?"

"Of course," I said. "I'll show you 'round."

Amy made for the basement door. "Not that way," I said as I opened the front door, "come around the house." My heart pounded for a moment but I managed to sound casual. After all, visitors don't usually demand to see their host's basement. My rehearsed line, if anyone asked, was that I rented the space out for storage so it was locked up.

My raised beds that I had built myself with railway ties looked green and lush. Amy was full of admiration. "I wish I could grow vegetables," she said, "but we don't have enough room where the sun is." She took a slug of wine.

Yeah, I thought, and you don't want to get your hands dirty. "I'll give you a cauliflower when they're a bit bigger," I said.

"Great. I'm not used to fresh produce. Never have been."
She sighed. "I grew up in a house where the garden was always
full of old cars and junk."

I stooped to pull a weed.

"I couldn't wait to get out of that place," Amy continued.
"It was a dump. And my mother was a slob. All she could
cook was hamburger. Hamburger, day in, day out." She tilted
her head and threw the rest of the wine back. I half expected
her to toss the glass over her shoulder, but she didn't. "Yes, a
slob. A big, fat slob. Smoked. Non-stop. Cigarette butts all
over the house. Burn marks on the kitchen counters." She
shuddered and then nearly tripped, but saved herself by
clutching on to me.

It must have been the wine—her esses were decidedly
slushy. I had never heard her talk like that, but then I had to
confess I had never asked her about her childhood. Nor had I
seen her so relaxed. It must have been Swan's influence.

Still holding on to my arm she said, "You've never liked
me, have you?"

I didn't know what to say. Tell her how right she was?
Instead I managed, "What makes you think that?" I moved
away from her and she nearly fell over.

"I'm not good enough for your son, am I?" She grabbed
my arm again. "Am I? And I don't bring up the children right,
do I? I'm not 'fraightfully jolly,' not 'stiff upper lip,' not good
enough. But I tell you what—your son loves me."

She let go of my arm and, swaying slightly, made for the
fence of runner beans.

"I think you make a good wife for Jason," I said. "Even
though you're not a Yorkshire woman. But you can't help that.

I don't suppose Yorkshire maidens were plentiful in the interior of British Columbia." I laughed, but Amy didn't seem to find it funny. I had never seen Amy tiddly before. It was the most fun I'd ever had with her. I'd have to start bringing wine to Sunday dinners.

Amy reached for a bean and looked as if she were going to topple. I went over and began to pick beans too, but I didn't have anything to put them in.

"I don't really want you to live with us, you know." Amy shook her head more than was necessary so that a lock of hair fell over her eyes. She brushed it to one side. "Are you surprised?"

"You were just being kind."

"Not for you," she said hastily. "For Jason's sake. He's worried about you." She handed me her beans, examined her glass, and tipped it into her mouth even though it was empty. "We can't afford to keep you, you know. Not when the children's schooling is coming up."

It was time to put a stop to her. "Look Amy, I don't bloody well expect you to keep me or look after me, so get off my case. And we don't have to be all lovey-dovey to get along, so you put up with me and I'll put up with you, right?"

She swayed slightly and looked at my beans. "I'll get you one of those flat baskets," she said. "For produce. They have them in Kootenai Moon. I must remember next time I'm in town."

As we wandered back inside, Amy said, "I've been thinking. Perhaps Nicholas could come here to play while I take Julie to the library."

"That would be wonderful," I said and meant it. "What days would that be?"

"Wednesday mornings from ten to eleven. I'll drop him off."

Fun. I must re-stock the play chest.

We reached the front door and Amy said, "Swan's smart isn't she?"

"Smart?"

"Bright. She's very intelligent."

Fortunately I had my back to her. Swan intelligent?

The amount of time I spent on the computer increased daily as I learned how to search, where to look things up, and organizations to join so that I received their newsletters. After I'd plucked up courage to put 'marijuana growing' in the Search box, I was amazed at the number of results there were. After the first time I saw the pictures of the varied and colorful plants, I went downstairs to water and stared at my buddies. Compared with the pictures, they presented a sorry sight. They should have been sturdy and upright with firm, large buds but they were straggly with drooping soft buds. The canes helped to hold them up a little, but next time I would use tomato cages.

Although I had been careful about snipping off the flowering shoots that seemed to spring up overnight, there were still too many that had escaped and turned into tiny buds. Growing pot needed more skill than I had. It wasn't just a few plant pots in the basement, but what soil, type of food, the PPM of the food, how to prune, type of lighting, how much water. The list went on and on. The computer would be a great help and then, of course, there was my garden sage, Michael to help me master the art of growing.

Should I write to Lisa about my garden? She was a botanist and knew about plants, particularly tropical ones, but she might be shocked that her mother was a criminal. If she had been home it would be different because she would stay with me and I would have to come clean.

I never thought about looking for work anymore. I imagined applying for a job.

"So you've been a nurse's aide and a waitress. What are your ambitions?"

"To grow pot with magnificent buds. Big enough to knock your socks off."

17

AT LONG LAST harvest day arrived, and with it the prospect of some money. Swan had been round to check the plants. "Hmm," she said, "the buds could be bigger but they're nice and hard. Spider mites didn't help."

She told me what to get ready: chairs for two trimmers and one for me if I was going to trim, a good light, lines to hang the buds on to dry, snacks and lunch for everyone, heavy-duty garbage bags, a jar of rubbing alcohol to put the scissors in to take the gunk off, and some sort of tray for each trimmer to work on. I already knew I was to pay $20 an hour to each trimmer, but they could wait until I got paid if necessary. It was necessary.

"Me and Marcus will bring our own scissors," Swan said.

"Will he be back in time?"

"He says he will. I'll find someone else if he's not around."

"How long will it take?"

Swan thought for a moment. "Four lights…we can probably finish in one day. Maybe two if there are a lot of small buds."

We were in the basement when we made these plans. Lack of space became a problem when we discussed where we would sit. If we used the area near the water heater and furnace, the light was poor and we would be scattered; if we used the space at the foot of the stairs, we couldn't move; the space next to the new wall meant we would be sitting in a row, so the only place was near the back door where I had stacked the garbage bags.

"I don't know where to put these," I had said to Swan, pointing at the garbage.

"No prob. We'll move them into the grow room just before we start."

She was so nonchalant, while I was gearing up for a fit of acute anxiety. Her hand-on-the-doorknob warning had been, "Don't forget the whole house will stink. Burn incense."

I took down three folding chairs, two angle-poise lamps, and two small tables, but I couldn't set them up until the garbage bags were out of the way, so I just left them ready. I did manage to run string lines for the buds around the furnace area, but I had no idea how many or at what height. And three lids from storage boxes in the spare room could act as trays.

On the big day the house smelled like a Buddhist temple after I'd lit a whole package of Nag Champa incense, something I don't normally use. I hoped no one I knew would visit, but that was unlikely at nine o'clock in the morning. So I froze when there was a knock at the door shortly before nine. Swan perhaps? But she was usually late. A delivery? I hadn't ordered anything. Who could it be?

I opened the door a crack and peered out. Maggie stood on the doorstep.

I stared at her. Should I pretend I'm not home? Should I pretend I'm sick? No, she'd be worried about me. I'll have to just try to get her away as fast as possible. I opened the door.

"Oh, hi Maggie. How nice to see you. But I'm afraid this isn't a good time. I'm just rushing out."

"I really need to talk to you. Can we have coffee?" Maggie stepped into the hall.

I didn't know what to do. Swan would arrive any moment, but surely she would see I had a visitor and not expect to continue. We could always delay the business and mercifully, the only smell was of incense.

I hesitated then said, "Sure, I'll put the kettle on." I'd always thought that being a loyal friend is important no matter what the circumstances, but this time I just wanted Maggie to vanish.

"My god, it smells in here," Maggie said. "Have you turned into a Buddhist?"

I shook my head. Was she going to stay long? How could I make her leave?

Maggie had a look of sheer delight on her face. "It's okay, Jess. I'm here to trim."

"What!" I nearly keeled over with surprise. Maggie. A trimmer. I stared at her with wide eyes.

"Marcus has been held up, so Swan asked me to come. I thought the address she gave me seemed familiar but it wasn't until I got here that I realized it was you," Maggie began to take off her shoes.

"Oh, leave your shoes on—we're going into the basement," I said.

Maggie straightened up. "Well, well, Jess. Who would have thought it?"

"I'm just as surprised to see you."

We smiled at each other and then began to laugh. Then we hugged. "Partners in crime," I said. "I wish I'd known sooner, I could have used a mate."

"I brought a casserole for our lunch. I always do. It's often young guys who can't boil an egg, let alone make lunch." Maggie said. "It needs to go in the oven an hour before we eat."

"Bless your heart—you didn't need to do that."

Another knock on the door heralded Swan. "Oh you've met Maggie," she said.

"Maggie and I are old friends. I wish I'd known she did this. How do you two know each other?"

"Trimming," Swan said.

It turned out that Maggie had been growing for about five years and through Marcus, Swan started trimming for her shortly after her arrival in Nelson. Swan had never done it before, so she had learned the tricks of the trade from Maggie.

"I won't be growing much longer," Maggie said. "I'm saving up so I can take three years off to go to school. I'm nearly there." She gripped her hands and raised them like a winning boxer.

I made everyone coffee and we headed downstairs. My heart sang. Maggie, whom I really liked, was a companion in my adventure. All my anxieties dissipated as I prepared to enjoy the day. Swan and Maggie took over; they moved the full garbage bags, set up the chairs and the lamps, opened a new garbage bag, and arranged a table for their scissors and water glass. My job, I was told, was to cut the plants and bring them in a few at a time, hang up the trimmed buds, and tidy up as we went along. If I wanted to learn how to trim, that would be fine, but they could do it all.

I silently thanked each buddy as I cut her off at her base with a pair of garden clippers and carried each bushy plant in to Swan and Maggie. I needed another container to put the untrimmed plants in so I dashed out to the garage to get a cardboard box.

I was closing the side door of the garage when Kate, the woman who lived across the lane, came over. Why then? I hardly ever spoke to her. I tried to look pleasant as she said, "Good morning, Jess. I hope you are well."

"Yes, I'm fine. You?" I tried not to look impatient.

"I'm looking for volunteers for a fund-raising effort to raise money to provide water wells in one part of rural Africa. Would you be interested?" Kate had one of those kind, open faces that emit sympathy and I hated to refuse her.

I put the box down and the movement produced a pungent smell from the over shirt I wore in the grow room and that I hadn't thought of removing before rushing out. "I don't have much money, I'm sorry," I said.

"I'm looking for your time. Would you man a stall for four hours at the bazaar we're holding next month? In the church hall."

"I can do that," I said. "I'd like to know more about the

organization." Why I said that I'll never know as Kate then told me all about WaterCan, a charity that funds projects to create sustainable clean water in four East African countries. "I'll drop off some flyers," she said finally.

It must have been at least twenty minutes before I returned to the basement.

"We thought you'd got lost," Maggie said.

"I bumped into a neighbor I hardly ever see. I'm sure she could smell me."

Maggie and Swan sat under a light with a bin lid on their laps either pulling at leaves or trimming buds. With comparative darkness around them and with a spotlight illuminating them as they hunched intently over a plant, they reminded me of an oil painting I'd seen somewhere—Guy Fawkes plotting perhaps?

They were both remarkably quick: buds turned, scissors flashed, and before long there was quite a collection of trimmed buds ready for me to hang on the lines I had strung.

"So Marcus introduced Swan to you, Maggie? How do you know Marcus?"

"Oh I've known him since he was a baby. Watched him grow up." She frowned. "These buds are too small and there shouldn't be so many of them on one branch. Your pruning needs work."

"I know. I didn't learn how to prune until it was too late. I thought Marcus would show me."

"Marcus is not the greatest indoor grower. It's outdoors he knows."

"Right. That's why he's away most of the summer isn't it?" I stood there like a bump on a log. "What was he like as a kid?"

"Average student. Energetic. Played soccer. Outdoorsy. Loved mountains." Maggie peered at the bud she had just trimmed before tossing it into a box and picking up another plant.

I wanted to sit down with them and help. "Please show me how to trim."

Swan handed me an extra pair of scissors she had brought. They showed me how to cut off a branch, strip off the leaves, and then cut all around the bud until it was smooth but not shaved. "You leave a bit of branch so you can hang them up," Swan told me.

"How did you meet Marcus, Swan?" I asked.

"Mutual friend. It's too bad about his accident. What happened, Maggie?"

"He took up rock climbing in a big way. He became really good. I watched him once at a demo. He looked like Spiderman. He'd just started electrician training at Selkirk when they went down to Joshua Tree and he had a fall. He broke a wrist. At first no one figured he'd hit his head." Maggie shook her head and picked up another plant.

"What happened?" Swan asked.

"They fixed his wrist of course, and examined him. The doctor asked about his head but he didn't remember hitting it. He seemed okay, but then his parents noticed he couldn't concentrate for more than a few minutes at a time. He went back to school but he couldn't handle the school work." Maggie pushed hair out of her eyes with her wrist.

"Can't they find out what's wrong?" I asked.

"They did all sorts of tests and scans and couldn't find anything. I tried homeopathy on him and there was some improvement at first, then he seemed to stop. But he's functional. He just doesn't communicate very well."

"I'll say," Swan said. "He shuffles around at parties not talking. Girls think he's creepy."

"Poor lad," I said. "Where does he live?"

"With his parents," Maggie said. "His dad's an electrician so Marcus sometimes works with him."

"Does his dad know he sets up grow rooms?"

Maggie laughed. "I doubt it. They're both pillars of the community."

My first efforts at trimming were very slow and clumsy compared with my skilled friends and I was quite glad of the breaks when I stood up to clip more plants or to hang up the buds or to stuff leaves on the floor into a garbage bag.

"What does the future hold for Marcus?" I asked Maggie.

"I wish I could say it's bright, but no one knows. He's been to a neurologist in Kelowna and I think Don and Mary want to send him to the Mayo clinic or somewhere like that, if they can find the bucks. I know I could help him. If only I knew more." Maggie ripped leaves off a plant in frustration.

What if I made a fortune from my garden? I could send Marcus off to be cured. But cured of what? Not talking? No, so he could go back to school and do what he wanted to do.

"When's he back?" Would Marcus be back in time to sell my crop?

"In a few days," Swan said. "He'll be back before your buds are ready."

"I've been looking at pictures of plants on the Internet," I said. "I hadn't realized there's such a variety. What sort are these?"

"Jamaican," Swan said. "They're the easiest to grow. There's Hemp Star, but they smell more."

"I heard there's a new one called God," Maggie said. "Supposed not to smell at all."

"Wicked," Swan said. "I wonder how easy it is to grow."

I left them for a short time while I went upstairs to put the casserole in the oven. My brief respite made me realize how smelly it was downstairs and how rank I was. Kate must have smelled me if her nose was in good working order. Both Swan and Maggie had changed their top clothes before starting but I hadn't. I hoped the incense would do the trick but anyway, if anyone came to the door I wouldn't answer it.

It was a lovely day and we had lunch on the deck. "It's a pity we can't work out here," I said as I took a deep breath of fresh air.

"I know someone who lived out of town and they decided to trim outdoors," Maggie said. "What they didn't know was that a retired police officer lived across the river from them. He was fond of bird watching and saw them through his binoculars. Next thing my friend knew, one of the Finest showed up."

"What happened?"

Maggie finished her mouthful of food. "He was told to dismantle his equipment and quit. So he did."

"He didn't get charged?"

"No. The police hate having to dismantle a grow op, so if it's just a mom-and-pop operation, they sometimes let it go," Maggie said. "My friend is hardly the criminal type."

"There was a bust up the road recently," Swan said. "They weren't so lucky. Mind you, they found hard drugs in the house and a gun. Come on, let's get back to work."

"How did the police know?" I asked.

"It was a house near where they check for seat belts," Swan said. "They could smell it. The guy needed a new filter and hadn't bothered. Some people are morons. Ask to get caught. I'd be pissed if I got caught because of someone else's stupidity."

I cleaned up the kitchen while the others went downstairs. I mustn't become too cavalier; it could happen to me. What would I do if a cop showed up? I was not going to live with that fear. We have too much fear in our society without me joining in.

We stopped for a cuppa and finally finished about 6:30. Swan promised to drop by the next evening and help me empty the plant pots into bags and load them into the car. Maggie said she would help me deal with the dry buds in a few days. "When they're nearly dry you need to twig them. That means cutting off the dry stalks and any other bits," she said.

Maggie told me to lay out the twigged buds on a tray or on cardboard. I had an under-bed storage box—that would do. She would come back when they were dry to weigh and pack them into large Ziploc plastic bags.

"I guess I should move the buds upstairs before I fumigate the basement to get rid of the spider mites?" I said before she left.

"Is that what you're going to do?"

"Michael told me to leave the lights on for three days and then let off a Doctor Doom. But I don't want to kill off my seedlings or ruin the buds."

"Good idea. I don't know why Marcus wasn't more

careful. Anyway, it's always a good idea to clean out your room between grows."

"Thanks, Maggie. I'm so glad you're in on this. Makes me feel better."

I went back downstairs to clean up a bit, but then I felt so weary I watched TV instead. That night my dreams were of lush jungle plants with huge glossy leaves and mighty flowers that glowed in the dark. I reached out to pick one, but a striped snake reared out from between the petals and hissed at me. I ran away in terror and found myself crouching behind a furnace before I woke up.

18

TIME FLASHED BY as it does when you're busy. Not only was there much work downstairs, but my outdoor garden also kept me busy. Harvest time meant my canner was on a permanent boil as I bottled beans and tomato sauce and peaches from the Okanagan. I never understood why they call it 'canning' here when they use jars, not cans, but then there were a lot of things I could never understand. Like why marijuana was illegal but gin was not. At this thought I sang Flanders and Swan's, "Have some Madeira, m'dear. It's really much nicer than beer. For the evil gin does would be hard to assess; besides it's inclined to affect my prowess, so have some Madeira, m'dear."

My cheerfulness arose from the thought that I would soon have some money. I didn't know how much, but I did know that the first thing I would do would be donate to the food bank and the second, renew my subscription to the Foster Parents Plan. I would try to get Sonali, my former foster child, back. And I would take Swan and Maggie out for a nice lunch—and Marcus, if he would come—and I would treat the Crones to croissants with their coffee, and I would… Get off it, you have to live for three months before the next crop and besides, you might not make much. And wouldn't people wonder why you were suddenly flush?

Swan came over in the morning to help take the bags of old soil to the dump. It had been quite strenuous emptying all the pots into garbage bags and then lugging them out to the car along with the bags of leaves. We had done this late the night before, after I'd made sure the neighbor's lights were off.

The car stank to high heaven. Whatever I did, I must not have an accident or be stopped, so I drove as if I had a spud stuck up my tail pipe—which is how many old people drive anyway. There was one road, near me, where the police often made seat belt checks. I avoided it and zigzagged through the side streets until we reached downtown, and then we took the road along the lake to the dump.

I was determined to stay calm, to play it cool, as they say, to treat this experience as normal. After all, people drop stuff at the dump all the time. Why should I be any different?

My palms were sweaty when I drove on to the scale. A woman poked her head out of her booth and asked, "Household?"

My voice quavered as I said, "No. Pot plants."

She roared with laughter as she pointed us to a bin. "Ask a silly question, eh?"

As we drove across to the Household dumpster, Swan looked at me incredulously. "What the hell did you say that for?"

"Just having a bit of fun. I don't know what came over

me." I do have a tendency to crack jokes at inappropriate times, particularly when I'm nervous.

"That wasn't funny."

"You're right."

A man in an orange vest came to help. Swan waved him away. "Thanks. We're okay," and began to unload the car. It was soon empty and as we drove away the most enormous relief swept over me. Yet another challenge mastered.

"In any other town the dump would be out in the boonies, not on the lake," I said to Swan. She had gone all silent on me. "What's the matter?"

"If you do that again, I'm not coming with you." She turned toward me, a look of fury on her usually serene face. "I don't want to get busted because you're too dumb to get that what we're doing is illegal." Her voice rose to a crescendo. "Illegal. Bad. GET IT?"

"Yes, I'm well aware it's illegal. But if governments make silly laws, it's up to citizens to ignore them."

"Fine for you to say. They'd never put you in jail, you're too old." Swan turned to her side window, her left shoulder lifted against me.

"They wouldn't put you in jail either. You don't grow." I pulled up at a Stop sign and let pedestrians cross.

Swan swivelled to face me. "What do you know? If I get busted, I'll be deported."

By this time I was so unnerved I didn't really hear what she said. "If you don't want to get caught, you shouldn't dress like a homing device for cops," I said.

Her eyes widened. "What? You ungrateful cow. You wouldn't be able to grow if it wasn't for me."

I was so shaken I pulled over. Before I had time to speak, she hissed, "Why don't you go to the cop shop and tell them what you're doing? Just as a joke."

"I'm sorry, Swan. I didn't mean…"

"You don't have a fucking clue," she said as she opened the door, got out, slammed it, and strode off.

I remained parked and stared at the blur in front of me. It was some time before my numb body could engage the gears and drive home. The voice in my head yattered: *Silly old fool, Swan's right, you are useless. You couldn't manage without her. What did you say that for? About how she dresses. Stupid, that's what you are.*

I parked so badly in my garage that I couldn't open the door so I had to back out and try again. That time the side mirror took a swipe.

A cup of tea was all I could think of when I got in, but as soon I entered the hall I heard a noise downstairs. Then footsteps. I unlocked the inside basement door and Marcus appeared.

"I turned off the lights," he said.

"Hello, Marcus. Welcome back." We stared at each other. I hardly recognized him. His hair, bleached by the sun to a streaky blond, had grown to a length that he could tie in a ponytail. His skin could have belonged to a South Sea islander he was so tanned, but his eyes were the same intense brown and his stare was as unnerving as usual.

Typically, he didn't look as if he was about to say anything. Suddenly, my sorrow over Swan turned to anger at him. "Kindly turn them back on. I left them on for a reason."

I stormed into the kitchen and put the kettle on. He

followed and hovered looking almost hangdog. "Hey," he managed to say.

"I left the lights on so I can get rid of the bloody spider mites you gave me." I thumped my purse on the kitchen table. Swan had left her bag; a colorful, handmade cotton one, hung over a chair. Good, I thought, that will give me a reason to call her.

"How come?" Marcus mumbled.

"Leave the lights on for three days with no extraction fan and then set off a Doctor Doom. I learned that from Michael because I learned bugger all from you." I'd already upset one young friend—now I was about to upset another.

He pressed both hands against the doorjambs and rocked himself from side to side. I carried on doing small chores that didn't need doing, like wiping the counters and shuffling things around.

Marcus suddenly stood up straight. "Your buds are nearly ready. Phone when they're packed," he said and left through the basement. I went to the top of the stairs and heard the hum start.

It should have been an exciting time, but it wasn't. I had to take any life forms out of the basement before fumigating it, so I dragged myself up and down two flights of stairs to the spare bedroom carrying trays of baby buddies in their fiber pots and the drying buds that I took down from the lines and put in a box. They had shrivelled so much that they seemed minute, not like I had imagined from the pictures on the Internet. They were as pathetic as I was.

Back downstairs, I rescued my cameo brooch and told Ceres I was moving her out of the room in case Dr. Doom did nasty things to her, but that I would put her back to oversee the next crop. Then I took the canister and read the instructions. I was to pull a tab, put it on the floor and get out. Could I manage that without doing something silly?

With trembling hands I pulled the tab. A jet of vapor hissed into my face before I stood the can up and ran out. Now I'd probably get a lung infection.

Closing the basement door brought the same sense of relief I had felt at the dump. The dump. Swan. I had left a message on her voice mail to say her bag was here. I would have taken it to her, but I wasn't sure exactly where she lived. I badly wanted to see her and apologize for being such an idiot. If I lost her out of my life I would miss her. Not just because she helped with the garden, but also because I had grown fond of her. She kept me in touch with life, with youth, and with my sense of humor. Without her I would hardly see a soul. Poverty means a deprived social life—you can't afford to entertain or have coffee or meals out.

I made myself go upstairs to twig the buds. It was a nice, easy job sitting and cutting off stalks and bits of leaf in the sunny spare bedroom, and I began to feel more chipper. I had learned so much in the four months since Marcus had built the room: how to manage the lights, how to feed, trim, and harvest the plants, and soon, how to weigh and pack the final product. The buds were dry, but I spread them out on an under-the-bed storage bin anyway. I phoned Maggie who said she'd be over in the morning with her scale and to make sure I bought some large Ziploc bags.

The cuttings, on the floor under the window, really needed to be transplanted as they were getting straggly. "Not long now," I told them, "then you'll be in nice big pots and you can spread your roots." According to the book, they should go into progressively bigger pots, but I planned to plant them straight into the two gallons. I had had a brain-wave when I bought the four-inch pots to transfer the jiffies into: instead of plastic, I got the fiber ones that break down in soil so you can just transplant the seedling, pot and all, and not disturb the roots.

There was nothing more to do. Pots needed to be filled with soil, but there wasn't any; besides, the pesticide needed twelve hours to dissipate before I could go into the basement. It was raining, so I couldn't garden outside. I turned to the TV and watched a stupid movie about monster plants that terrorized the nearby town until our Hero arrived and killed them with a tuning fork. They shrivelled at a certain decibel of sound.

Next day the doorbell rang early. The woman on the porch was built like a brick shithouse, as my father used to say. If you ran into her, you would bounce and she would remain unmoved. She wore a heavy, beige masculine raincoat with a belt, even though it wasn't raining, and she vigorously shook a black umbrella before saying, "Good morning."

"Good morning," I said. She seemed vaguely familiar.

Then I remembered where I'd seen her: haranguing the crowd at the fire and another time, carrying a placard on Baker Street warning everyone of God's Revenge if they didn't turn to him.

Her grim face glowered at me. With that expression she looked like something that would eat its young. "I've come to talk about Jesus."

"Oh yes."

"Is he important in your life?"

"No, I believe he died more than two thousand years ago."

"Indeed. But his love lives on for those who mourn under the burden of sin. I proclaim the Holy Way to find water so you never thirst again, to find bread—"

I began to close the door. "Speaking of thirst, I could do with a cuppa. Bye." The woman stepped forward so that if I shut the door it would bang in her face. "You said you wanted to talk about Jesus, but really, you want to talk so that I have to listen. Well, thanks, but no thanks," I said firmly.

"Are you a sinner?" she asked, her face only inches from mine, one foot holding the door open.

"Definitely. Have been all my life. How about you?" I was beginning to panic, sure that I had a candidate for mental health services on my hands. Suppose she wouldn't leave, what would I do?

"Repent, so that you may enter the Garden of Paradise." Her blue eyes widened as her face assumed a righteous expression. "For Jesus welcomes you into his garden, where everything is filled with his divine nature. But to be in his presence, we must become pure through death of our sinful natures."

"Right. I'll work on it." I tried kicking her foot away and closing the door, but she seemed oblivious to my efforts.

"To be freed from sin, you must believe and hope in God's promise. You must ask yourself how well you tend your earthly garden, otherwise you too will perish in the wilderness without ever entering the promised land—the heavenly garden."

"Yes, well I'm doing my best to tend my earthly garden." I pushed on the door as hard as I could but I couldn't budge her.

"You okay, Jess?" A merciful heaven intervened in the form of Maggie. She elbowed the woman aside with an "Excuse me," came through the door and shut it forcefully.

I quickly locked it. "Am I ever pleased to see you! That woman is a nutcase."

"Yes, I heard her."

"I didn't know what to do. I couldn't shut the door and if I left for the phone I think she would have followed me." I peered through the stained glass pane in the front door. "She's still there."

"She'll go soon. I'm early, I know, but I have to leave early. I've brought the scales. It won't take long." Maggie took off her jacket and hung it over the banister rail.

"They're upstairs because I fumigated the basement," I said. "And the long storage bin is too difficult to shift."

In the spare bedroom, I pulled out the bin and took a deep breath to inhale the aroma of dried buds, a quite different smell than growing plants, and very pleasant. Maggie unboxed a flat scale on top of the dresser and weighed an empty Ziploc bag while I poured the coffee I had ready.

"Have you seen Swan lately?" I asked as casually as I could.

"Not since we trimmed here." Maggie began to stuff handfuls of buds into the Ziploc. "Some people are super careful packing but I just stuff them in."

"She left her bag here and I can't get hold of her. I've looked in the deli, but she's not been there."

"You want 227 grams, which is half a pound, plus two-and-a-bit grams for the bag." Maggie looked up at me. "I expect she'll show. She may have gone to trim for the outdoor guys."

"Oh. She didn't say." I tried to take an interest in the packing and weighing. "So you fill a bag and then remove or add buds to get 230 grams?"

"Yes. Did you want help with something?"

"No. Not really."

Maggie must have guessed from my tone or lack of enthusiasm for the proceedings that something was wrong, but she went on weighing until six half-pound bags plus a handful of extra buds lay in the bin.

"Three pounds. Not bad for a first effort." She sat on the bed with her coffee.

"What do I do with the extra?"

"You could smoke it. Or make brownies. Or keep it and add it next time."

"I've never smoked pot. Or cigs for that matter. Not since I was a teenager. I've tried, but I can't inhale. Makes me cough." I patted the six plastic bags filled with dried bud. "I still would like to try, but I don't even know how to roll a joint."

"You don't need to. You can get yourself a vaporizer so

you inhale steam, not smoke. Much healthier that way." Maggie stretched her legs. "What's up with Swan?"

"I did something really silly and she went off in a huff and I haven't seen her since." I sat on the only chair. "I feel terrible."

"What happened?"

"We drove to the dump with the dead plants and leaves and when the woman asked what we had, I went and said pot. The attendant thought it was funny, but Swan was furious."

"I expect you frightened her."

"Yes, she said she'd be deported if she was caught. I didn't know she's an American."

"She's from California. Berkeley. Her parents are professors at the university there."

I was amazed. "Lordy. They must be shocked by their offspring."

"Oh, I don't know about that. Swan is unusual. And very bright. I think they're wise enough to let her find herself."

I was taken aback by Maggie's opinion of Swan. I had only seen her as flighty, a bit daft, and unable to think of anything but boyfriends. I remembered that Amy had thought her intelligent.

Maggie continued, "Pot growing is a risky business, Jess. Kids like Swan can't afford to get a criminal record."

"I guess not."

Where did politicians get off? Deciding that marijuana was harmful but liquor was not and proclaiming to ordinary people what they could and could not grow?

"I'll be seeing Marcus later. I'll tell him you're ready." Maggie stood up and put her mug on the tray. "Got to go."

"How long does he take to sell it?"

"Depends on who's in town. Sometimes he's back in an hour or two and sometimes it's a few days."

"Thank you so much, Maggie. I owe you, and Swan, for trimming. As soon as I get the dollars I'll be in touch. Oh, and will you tell Marcus I need soil?"

Maggie opened the front door and a voice said, "Repent, so that you may enter the Garden of Paradise." Maggie quickly closed the door. "Phone the police. I'll go out the back."

"Do you really think I should ask the police to come here?"

"They won't come in. They'll just deal with the woman."

"But if they do come in, what do I do? I expect the place stinks. I better burn incense."

"Candles are better. It didn't stink when I came in." Maggie headed for the basement.

I lit candles in the living room, then phoned the local police and told them I had a religious nutcase on my porch who wouldn't go away.

"That'll be Eliza. She's harmless. But we'll send someone over to take her home."

One of the things I liked about Nelson was its tolerance for eccentrics: strangely dressed people on Baker Street, a man who kept bicycles on his roof, a man who wore a blanket and carried a wooden staff, and all the incredible hair dos, tattoos, and piercings. This sort of tolerance seemed to provide a rich soil for artists to grow in—as well as other things.

I moved the seedlings and the packaged buds downstairs to keep the smell in one place, a place with an air vent. Three pounds; at two thousand dollars a pound that would be six thousand, and half of that would be mine. Three *thousand* dollars. Now that has to last three months, I told myself, so that's one thousand a month, so be careful. The following month, I would start getting Old Age Security and that would be about a thousand a month. Two thousand a month; two thousand. I could manage very nicely on that.

To get going on the next crop meant some hard work for a while. I needed soil to fill the pots and start again and I kicked myself for not telling Marcus that while he was here. I carried everything back downstairs, put the packaged buds on the shelf next to the seedlings and switched on the air vent. As I left the cupboard I noticed two bales of soil near the back door. Marcus must have brought them the day before. He had his uses after all.

19

I WAS BEGINNING to feel I had a split personality, like Jekyll and Hyde. Half of me was an upright citizen doing the things I'd always done, like meeting with the Crones and my family, and the other half was growing pot in my basement. Each activity meant moving in quite different circles and having to adjust to each. In what I thought of as my ordinary life, I talked about the weather, local politics, and my grandchildren. As a gardener, topics of conversation were soil, pruning, and plant food. Neither circle overlapped. Maggie was the only common denominator.

Everyone knows what it's like when your thoughts are elsewhere, yet you have to act as usual. I was like that in both roles. As a pot grower it was, what the hell am I doing? What would happen if I were caught? Was I was doing it right? In my ordinary life I was a fugitive who had something to hide and was always on my guard.

The people in each circle were so different too. My gardening friends were young, laid back and spoke a language I barely understood. To them I was older, yes, but they didn't hold it against me. In fact they listened to me, and Marcus thought I was funny. My ordinary friends were, well, just the same: same attitudes, same values, same daily routine and comfortable with it all. That's what got on my nerves—the complacency.

The Company of Crones decided to meet in Lakeside Park because we were enjoying an Indian summer and we wanted to take advantage of it before we had to hunker down for the long winter ahead. We met at the picnic tables under a shelter and, instead of bringing a bag lunch, most of us partook of the excellent food provided by the concession.

There was no plan for our meeting other than to walk the labyrinth that had been built near the shelter. The labyrinth was a metaphor for a journey to your inner self and then back to the outer world with a broader understanding of who you were. At least that's how it was explained to me. I can't say I had ever finished walking it with a revelation of my inner self, but maybe that was because I usually entered it when I was consumed with some problem. Quite often I had solved the problem after walking slowly in diminishing circles, but I was still the same old Jess at the end, no nearer Enlightenment than before.

Four women were there when I arrived. Shortly after, Thelma showed up, all in white: white flimsy shirt, white slacks, white sandals, and enormous white sunglasses. Her floppy straw hat set on her white hair and her bright red lipstick were the only contrast.

"How's tricks?" I asked her after greeting the others.

"George wants to come back." Everyone leaned forward. Six people, most of them hard-of-hearing, at a picnic table made conversation difficult.

"Chloe gave him the big brush off. So now he sits on his own at dinner." Thelma looked around at everyone with a satisfied smirk. "Serves him right." She stood up, took off her sunglasses, and with a lot of hip swaying and toe pointing sang,

"Let him go, let him tarry, let him sink or let him swim
He doesn't care for me nor I don't care for him
He can go and get another that I hope he will enjoy
For I'm going to marry a far nicer boy."

We all applauded. "Are you?" Jane asked. "Going to marry again, I mean."

Thelma managed to appear coy by looking down at the table and pursing her lips. "Maybe. Maybe not," she said.

Just then, a woman arrived, flamboyant in a flowered purple dress. I didn't recognise her until someone said, "You look well, Laura. Are you better?"

Good heavens, it was Laura! The last time I'd seen her was in the hospital looking like death warmed over. That was about three months earlier. She hadn't been at the last meeting when Thelma had told us about George, but someone had said she wasn't any better. So what had produced this remarkable transformation?

"Whatever did you do?" I asked.

Laura sat down. "Yes, I'm much better. It was my nephew who found the cure. He's a pharmacy student and did a work term here. He makes special little brownies for me. I'm only to eat one a day, at dinner time, and you wouldn't believe how much better I feel."

"What's in the brownies?" Maggie asked. She looked at me with eyes wide open and a slight nod, but I didn't pick up the message.

"I'm not sure. Some sort of medicinal plant. But he makes them just for me. They don't work with all the other pills I was taking, he said, so I've stopped those. And I feel great." Laura looked around smiling.

She did look great; she had put on weight, her eyes shone, and her skin bloomed. But the biggest change was in her outlook: she was positive, no longer a Moaning Minnie, less anxious and even serene.

"What are you going to do now he's gone back to school?"

"He's got a friend here who will make them and deliver them to me when I run out." She produced a container. "They help with conditions affecting the elderly, he says, so I've brought you all a brownie to try."

The container circulated and we each took a small cake that tasted of chocolate.

"I wonder if they'd make me feel better," Joan said. "My arthritis is getting worse. I can hardly move this shoulder, look." She lifted her left arm out straight and then tried her right arm, which couldn't rise.

"I'll see if Craig will make any more," Laura said. "Or find out where you can get them."

"We could go into business," Maggie whispered to me. So that was what was in the brownies? Geez, I was slow on the uptake.

"See if you can get us the recipe," I said to Laura. "We might be able to make them for ourselves."

"You didn't finish your story, Thelma," Jane said. "Are you going to marry again?" She turned to Laura. "You weren't here last time. George wants a divorce because he found out Thelma had an affair more than fifty years ago. So he went after Chloe, but now she's dumped him and wants to come back to Thelma."

We all smiled and looked at Thelma.

"I am dating, yes, but no thoughts of marriage. I'm having too much fun." Thelma nonchalantly waved a hand with bright red long nails.

"Who's the lucky chap?" I asked.

"He's younger than George and can still...you know..." Thelma said. "His name is Percy and he lives on the floor above me. Used to be an electrician."

My imagination took off. I pictured an elderly man in a dressing gown, with a walker, sneaking out of Thelma's apartment back to his own in the middle of the night and being caught by one of the staff.

"Just like your former lover," Joan said.

"Oh yes, but not as agile." Thelma smiled. "Good with his hands though," she said with a wink.

It was my turn to walk the labyrinth. Thelma's electrician wore a thick tartan dressing gown and even with a walker, he was sprightly. No, get rid of the walker. Have him bound up the stairs. I walked a few steps. Marcus had been to collect the buds and returned the same day with twenty-seven hundred in cash, not the three thousand I expected. My product had not reached the desired standard and only fetched eighteen hundred a pound. Why? The buds were too small and the quality wasn't good. What do dealers look for? Maggie might know. Swan. My little Swan. Marcus hadn't seen her and didn't know where she was. How could I have been so horrible? I wouldn't blame her if she decided to tell me to bugger off.

My eyes were teary when I reached the center of the labyrinth and began the return journey. If only I could tell her how sorry I was. I had to see her—I owed her a hundred and twenty dollars for trimming. I owed Maggie too, and I had the money with me. When I reached the end of the walk I wasn't a better person: I was still a stupid old fool.

Back at the picnic table I told everyone I was going to the concession and asked if I could bring anything back for anyone. Maggie jumped up and said she'd come with me. As we walked across the grass I managed to slip the money into her hand. "What I owe you for trimming. And Swan...you haven't heard from her, have you?"

"No. Don't worry, Jess. She'll show up."

"If she trimmed for the outdoor guys, she'd be back by now, wouldn't she?"

"The weather's been so good, they may have delayed the harvest for the buds to get bigger. Then she could have gone off for a few days camping or something."

We ordered and as we waited for our burgers and salads I admired the flowerbeds near the concession, still very colorful despite the fading of their summer glory, and still with enough fragrance to fill the air. A Japanese maple showed off its red-bronze leaves against the blue lake, and other deciduous trees tried to compete by turning their own leaves red. It's funny how the world appeared in glorious technicolor.

"So what do you think of Laura's recovery?" Maggie asked. "Is it really pot that's made her better?"

"No. Her nephew was smart to get her off her meds by saying they wouldn't work with his brownies, so it's stopping those that's improved her. The pot would make her more cheerful for sure."

I took the opportunity of being alone with Maggie to ask about quality of buds and why my return was less than expected.

"The buyers examine the buds closely and also smoke some. They seem to know what they want. I once got two hundred a pound more than the going rate based on the smoke."

"What did you do to make it so good?"

"That's what's so annoying—I don't know. I'd done what I'd always done. Didn't change the food, same sort of soil, same routine. Never did figure it out."

The server called our numbers and we picked up our orders. "It only happened once." Maggie said.

We moved to join the others. Thelma was telling a story about George and everyone seemed to find it hysterical, as they were giggling more than usual. I listened and found myself dissolving with mirth too, though I couldn't have told you why.

"And then he went down on bended knee to present Chloe with flowers, and guess what?" Thelma cracked up and couldn't speak. Finally she spluttered, "Silly old fool couldn't get up again."

We all shrieked with laugher. A couple walking past us stopped to stare.

"What happened?" someone asked.

"They had to send for the staff to help him, but they couldn't find anyone for at least fifteen minutes, so he was stuck there. Chloe got up and left him on his knees. When the staff came to get him on his feet, he'd seized up so much he couldn't walk and they had to get a wheelchair to take him to his room."

My stomach ached from laughing. I looked at my friends. What wonderful women. I wanted to go around and kiss each of them, but climbing over the bench of the picnic table was too much effort.

"Yeah, growing old is not for the faint of heart, my grandmother used to tell me," Claire said.

"There are some advantages," Maggie said. "A reporter asked a 104-year old what was the best thing about getting old and she said, 'No peer pressure.'"

Someone was sure to have a heart attack from laughing so hard, but everyone seemed inspired.

Joan said, "It's scary when you're old and you start making the same noises as your coffee maker."

Even old Nina joined in. "Someone wrote to the paper complaining about dogs on Baker Street and said, 'It's the dog's mess that I find hard to swallow.'" She was about to choke on her carrot stick but Maggie got up and patted her back.

"Back in olden days when Great Grandpa put horseradish on his head, what was he trying to do?" Maggie asked. We stared at her. With a straight face she said, "Get it in his mouth!"

Jane had one arm across her face. "Did you know it's impossible to lick your elbow?"

Everyone immediately contorted themselves in an effort to lick an elbow. Thelma even lay back from the bench, her toes tucked under the far side of the picnic table and her head on the ground, trying to reach her elbow that way. Then she couldn't move for laughing and we all had to heave her back up to sitting.

We were still giggling when an old and familiar man emerged from down the path toward us. As he came nearer someone said, "Isn't that Ed?"

"How did he know we were here?"

"I did the phoning," Claire said. "I left a message."

We fell silent. It was Ed. He'd come to tell us that we wouldn't be seeing Eva again. "She went off one night in her underwear. I was asleep and had forgotten to lock the door. It was all my fault." His rheumy eyes filled with tears. "If only I'd locked the door early. But I didn't."

"Is she all right?" someone asked.

"The police found her wandering down the highway. They took her to the hospital and she hasn't been home since."

I had a ridiculous desire to laugh at the image of Eva in her undies running down the highway. What on earth was the matter with me? Her plight was anything but funny.

The old man wiped his eyes with a cloth hanky. "They didn't know who she was, so they couldn't let me know. When I woke up and she wasn't there, I phoned the police and that's how I found out where she was. It's all my fault."

"Ed, you've done a wonderful job looking after her all this time," Maggie said. We all murmured agreement. "It's not your fault."

"I should have locked the door." He sniffed loudly. "She's

with our daughter in Chilliwack. I'm going there when I've sold our house."

"Are you both going to live with your daughter?" I asked.

"She's looking for a placement for Eva. I don't know what I'll do. I want to stay here and find a home for Eva here. Where all her friends are. Where I can see her every day. Trouble is, nursing homes for someone like Eva are too expensive and the regular ones are so understaffed the care is terrible."

The poor old fellow leaned on the picnic table looking the picture of dejection.

"Have you put her name down for Saint Mark's?" Joan asked. "I've heard good things about it."

"It's got a long waiting list. They all have. But people have to be…you know…mentally…" He wiped his eyes again.

"Do you need any help, Ed? You can always call on us, you know. We're not much good at lifting things, but we can help you by packing and making meals, right girls?" Maggie looked around.

"Right."

"You bet."

"That's very kind of you." His eyes filled again. "I just wanted to stop by and thank you for being so good to Eva. She always had a great time with you all. I'll tell her you said hello next time I see her."

"We'll send her a card. What's her address?" Maggie took over to get the details and then she helped Ed to his car as we all waved good-bye.

"God, I hope I don't end up in a Home," Thelma said.

"I thought you were in one," I replied.

"It's not a nursing home," she said firmly. "We've all got our marbles. And most of us can move. Except George when he can't get up off the floor." She tittered. "It's silly, but I sort of miss him. He was like having a puppy around—you get used to its presence. Now he's more hang dog than puppy after his little dalliance." She sighed. "Maybe I should lift him out of his misery. What do you all think?"

"Poor old bugger needs you," I said. "At least he's still romantic."

"Nursing homes aren't so bad if you can afford a good one," Laura said. "Poor Ed. He loves Eva so much. I wish I could afford to pay for her to come back so the old guy won't have to sell his house and move to the coast."

We had all sobered up after our hilarity. If only I had the money to help Ed and Eva. Maybe my garden would bring me riches?

20

TEN DAYS PASSED with no sign of Swan. When I called I got her voice mail and left a message to say I had the money I owed her. At the deli someone told me she was on vacation. At least she hadn't gone off because of me. Couldn't she have told me she was going to be away? Back to her old flakey ways. Just when I was getting fond of her.

A couple of mornings later, Swan showed up. She breezed in through the front door without knocking, calling out, "Hi, Jess. Howzit going?"

I wasn't sure what to expect when we finally met; coldness, tears, anger perhaps, but not carrying on as if nothing had happened. I ran to meet her in the hall. "Swan. I am *so* pleased to see you. I've been worried about you."

We hugged and then I held her away from me. "You look well. Really well."

Her skin glowed with suntan, her dark hair curled naturally and the lack of makeup emphasized her eyes. I hadn't noticed them before because she usually used so much mascara and shadow that she looked ready for the stage. They were stunning: light brown that reflected specks of gold and something else; intelligence. Had Swan been playing a part? The part of an empty-headed bimbo?

"My mother's been stuffing me with organic veggies and fruit."

"Oh, you've been home?"

"Yes. I got the call and I had to go, or else."

"Or else, what?"

"Trouble with a capital T."

Swan settled in a chair while I made coffee.

"You once asked where I was from, but I never told you. I'm from California. Berkeley. Yuck." She screwed up her face. "The place is full of nerds and geeks."

"You've lost your nose stud," I said.

"My mother made me take *it* out before she would take *me* out." Swan laughed. "It's great to be back. I feel like I've been in prison."

I plonked a coffee mug in front of her. "Swan, I've been feeling really bad about what I said to you. I am so sorry. You were right. I couldn't have started the garden without you and I am grateful. I had no cause to—"

"No worries," Swan said. "Forget it. You've been like a Mom to me, minus the bitching. It's cool."

There was silence for a while and then, "How's Sam?" I asked.

"Sam has a severe case of nonexistence. My new BF is more like a human." She stared out of the window for a while. "But it's not going anywhere. Anyway, I've gotta go home next summer."

"How come?"

"They gave me two years to get my act together. Then they want me to go to school and do something useful with my life." She said the last sentence in a falsetto, obviously imitating her mother.

I couldn't stop staring at her. It was as if she had undressed to reveal a different person, one I hadn't suspected was there. She had never tried to hide anything—I was the one who had taken her at face value, who had never asked questions to find out who she was, or what she thought. I had just assumed she was a flighty young lass with nowt much upstairs.

"What do you want to do?" I asked her.

"I needed time out. Didn't want to travel, just wanted to live in another place, get away from university geeks." She sighed. "Guess I'll have to go to school in the end, but I've got a few more months of freedom."

"What would you like to study?"

"Dunno. Not sure I want to go to school at all."

"Are you still working at the deli?"

"Part-time." She hesitated. "I'm going to start looking after your grandkids two days a week. Did Amy tell you? She wants to go back to work."

No, Amy hadn't told me. Why not? Why had I heard it from Swan when I'd only just been there for Sunday dinner? Bugger Amy.

Swan drained her coffee and stood up. "Gotta go."

"Let me get you the money I owe you." I saw her to the door.

"How's the garden?" she asked.

"Second crop. Three weeks into veg. Got rid of the spider

mites." I hesitated. "Tell me something. Is your name really Swan?"

She laughed at me. "If you met my parents you'd know the answer."

My second harvest was due and I expected to have some money to splurge on presents, and as usual I got carried away with imagining how far my money would go. The Crones always had a Christmas lunch at the Hume Hotel and I toyed with the idea of paying for everyone, but in reality, the money from the last crop had only lasted three months of normal expenses and I had very little left. When Marcus wasn't getting half my earnings, I could splash a bit.

It was nearing Christmas and time to think about presents for my grandchildren. I had knitted Nicholas a sweater, but that wasn't much fun for a five-year old to open, so I wandered downtown looking for ideas. The toyshop on Ward Street had me carried away with what I could buy the grandchildren. Julie would love a wooden crib for her doll and Nicholas, now into dressing up, would look a treat as a knight. Farther down Baker Street, I fell for a little picnic set in a sturdy basket.

I came to a shop I'd never been in before simply because the display of collector's metal signs, bumper stickers, huge sunglasses and baseball caps was such a mish-mash that I thought there would be nothing to interest me. But recent lessons in not taking things at face value made me wander in to take a closer look.

Cards with huge-breasted women in lewd poses reminded me of the postcards sold in British seaside towns in my childhood that were considered 'saucy' in my family and only to be giggled over at their stand.

Coffee mugs with pictures of Che Guevara balanced under flags waving peace symbols, posters of The Who and long-forgotten groups covered one wall, and stacks of old records that I used to play on my portable gramophone took up a large section at the back. When I came to the smoking apparatus my interest peaked. Glass cabinets displayed such an assortment of colorful glass pipes and other smoking devices that my eyes blinked. Large hookahs occupied an entire shelf while smaller ones mingled with the pipes, each one a work of art. Then I saw the vaporizers.

A young lass in an excuse for a skirt asked me if she could help. "Yes," I said, "I'm interested in a vaporizer."

She hesitated and looked at me as if wondering why this old biddy wanted a pot-smoking device.

I didn't know what to say. I hadn't the courage to think that it was none of her bloody business why I wanted a vaporizer, so I stood there with my mouth half open like an idiot.

The young woman smiled. "Did your Chinese medicine doctor prescribe some herbs that he said would be better smoked or inhaled in a vaporizer? That's usually why people want them."

I looked her in the eye and nodded.

"Ahh," she said and showed me two or three that worked on that principle. "You put your herb in the small bulb here, turn it on, and allow it to heat up. Then you draw in the vapor through this tube. This is the best one because it regulates the temperature." She indicated a wooden box with a tempera-ture gauge on it, "But this one is the cheapest."

The price meant I couldn't afford it that day, so I said, "Thank you. That looks just what I want. I'll come back in a few days."

Harvest day arrived. I knew what to expect. The house would stink, but the only hazard was someone walking in on me. I lit a couple of scented candles, as they seemed to mask the smell better than incense, and I wouldn't answer the door.

Swan and Marcus came to trim. This was a good time to get to know him better, but even Swan couldn't get him to utter more than a few words. His long fingers expertly trimmed buds with astonishing speed as he concentrated on what he was doing. What went on in his head? If he couldn't think straight he wouldn't be able to function, would he? What a waste of a beautiful young man.

"When you're tree planting, where do you stay, Marcus?" I tried a question to get him going.

"Camp," he said without stopping what he was doing.

"Do you have to take your own camping gear or is there a camp set up?"

"We take our own."

"Do you have to cook for yourself?"

"Camp cook."

"Is the food good?"

"It's okay."

And there ended the lesson according to Marcus.

Maggie thought it was just his speech center that was affected—that the thoughts were there, but he couldn't express them. If that was the case, couldn't something be done to help him? But why do we expect everyone to be chatty, to express themselves, to greet one another? Why should we think there is something strange about silence? Marcus obviously listened to people—why didn't I accept that as a blessing? After all, few people really listen to each other.

Swan and Marcus kept the radio on, otherwise there would have been almost complete silence. My hearing deficits couldn't stand the continuous noise, so I began to spend more time upstairs than downstairs. They didn't need me to trim anyway.

Marcus did make one comment of note. "Nice buds," he said. I thought so too. I had followed Michael's pruning directions and each plant grew only four buds. These were big, not as big as I had hoped, but they did make the trimming of the crop much quicker. By mid-afternoon Swan and Marcus had finished.

Swan helped me stack the car with garbage bags filled with expired pot plants and clippings and the next day we set off for the dump. I vowed to keep my mouth shut when we got there and not make smart-ass remarks.

As I drove carefully down Ward Street, a city police truck pulled out of a lane and settled behind me. "We're being tailed by a cop," I said to Swan.

She looked over her shoulder. "Yeah. Right."

I turned down toward the lake. The cop followed. Driving beside the airstrip, the police truck still following, I began to sweat. "What shall I do?" I said. "He's still behind me."

"You're not doing anything wrong," Swan said. "Keep going."

"I don't want him following me to the dump. I'll pull into the hardware store."

A distressed splutter from my car solved my problem. Two convulsive jerks and my engine died. Mercifully, it had enough poop left in it for me to glide onto the shoulder of the road.

The police truck passed me, then slowed, backed up and parked in front of me. Its driver's door opened. I stopped breathing, frozen to the seat.

"Quick, get out of the car," Swan urged as she unbuckled her seat belt, opened her door, and clambered out.

I did as she said and leaned on the car to support my legs that had lost their will to hold me up. A very large, pleasant-faced, older cop approached. "Are you in trouble? I saw your vehicle break down. Are you out of gas?"

"No, I don't think so," I said. I hoped he wouldn't notice the tremble in my voice. "It's an old car. Tends to do this. But don't worry, my friend has a cell phone and we can get some-one to rescue us."

The cop walked up to my door and peered in. "Your tank's full." He stood up and towered over me. "You sure you're okay?"

"Yes. Thank you so much for stopping. We'll be fine."

As he headed back to his truck Swan pulled out her cell. "I'll phone Marcus. If he can't get it going, we can unload into his truck." She turned to look at the lake. It's funny how when people use their cell phones they turn their backs on you.

I opened the car door to get in so I could sit down. The door was locked. In my panic I must have locked it. Ah well, the passenger door would do. It was locked too. Keys dangled invitingly from the ignition. My purse lay on the floor. "Bugger," I said loudly.

Swan turned to me. "I can't get hold of Marcus. I've left a message."

"We're locked out," I said.

"What did you lock your door for?"

"What did you lock *your* door for?"

We glared at each other over the car. Swan's wide eyes and strained face made me want to laugh. "That was a close shave," I said. "I'm still jelly."

We both relaxed and moved over to peer through the mesh fence separating us from the airstrip. "Now what do we do?" I said as we stared across to the lake. "We can't get a tow truck until we've emptied the car."

"Marcus might not be long. If he hasn't called soon, I know another guy who's cool." Swan shivered. Her coat lay on the back seat of the car.

"Let's walk back to that café back there and have a coffee while we wait," I said. Then, "Oh bugger, my purse is in the car. Have you got any money?"

Swan pushed her hands into her jeans pocket and pulled out ten dollars. "This'll do."

In the coffee shop, Swan called Marcus again to tell him where we were and we settled into the warmth. "You could try Maggie," I said. "If she's not around I can walk home to get the spare key. If we can dump the bags, it really doesn't matter how long the car sits there."

Although we were both shaken up after the encounter with the cop, there was really nothing to fuss about. Marcus showed up, drove me home for the spare key, took the bags to the dump, drove Swan and me home, and I got the car towed to a garage. End of story. But would my nervous system would ever recover? How much longer could I handle these close encounters with getting caught? Was growing worth it?

21

THE LARGE BUDS we harvested took longer to dry and it was close to Christmas before Maggie could come to weigh them. Four and a half pounds. Marcus got two thousand a pound for them that time, so I ended up with nine thousand to split with Marcus. With a light heart I went shopping again and bought the doll crib, the knight costume, the picnic basket, and a vaporizer for me.

The Crones celebrated Christmas together at the hotel, which provided restaurant service in a private room decorated for the season. We tried to capture the spirit by dressing in something festive and wearing sprays of holly or mistletoe. I wore my bright red sweatshirt with a glittery snowman and a reindeer on it, a sweatshirt that comes out once a year for this occasion. Some of us captured even more spirit with a gin and tonic.

We ordered lunch and did our 'check in' as we ate. To everyone's astonishment, Laura, instead of a new doctor-prescribed wonder pill, talked about the benefits of spirulina and the advantages of a serving of raw vegetables every day.

"Are you still taking your brownie every day?" I asked her.

"Oh yes. Craig checks up on me every week to make sure I have enough and to see how I am. I credit him with my recovery. Here's to Craig," she said and we all raised our glasses. "To Craig." Then "to Craig's brownies."

I talked about a wealthy aunt in England, then in her nineties and ailing. "I am her only living relative," I said. "Not that I'm holding my breath…" I raised my eyebrows and looked around the table.

My story was a complete fabrication. I did not have an old aunt, nor did I have any prospects of an inheritance, but I wanted to lay the groundwork to explain any increase in my income. Jason, always vague about his roots, was going to get the same story at some opportune moment. Perhaps when I got a lawyer's letter announcing my unexpected fortune? I would have to think about that, but at that moment I let the Crones know that my luck might change.

Thelma and George were back together. "He came to me with a bunch of flowers, all hang-dog and was about to go on bended knee when I encouraged him into a chair. He still loves me, always has, and thinks it's the new pill his doctor prescribed that sent him off balance. Silly old fool." She took a sip of gin. "But it's good to have him back. I've got used to him around and missed him when he wasn't there."

After we'd eaten we played our parcel game. Everyone brought a wrapped present and placed it under the tree in the room. We were to bring White Elephants, articles we didn't want or that had little value. Maggie gave everyone a slip of paper with a number on it. Nina, being the eldest, called out the first number and the holder of that number got first pick of a present. Then when she'd opened it, she called out the next number and so on. When it was your turn you could either take a new present or one someone else had chosen.

The present I had wrapped was a soft toy cow wearing pink pyjamas and with a silly grin on its face. Claire got it and then tried to persuade the next choosers to take it, but without success. Parcels that looked like books were usually a safe bet, but mine was *Finding Your Inner Caterpillar* and I couldn't find any takers for that either.

We were certainly filled with cheerful spirit when we left, and to walk some of it off I headed home via Baker Street and its side streets. I passed Bob's Café, which had a large For Sale sign in the window. Good thing I didn't get his job. I'd have been out of work again. And I would never have started my new business.

On Christmas Eve I unpacked my vaporizer and prepared to start the festive season feeling…what? I had asked Swan what it felt like to be high on pot, but she was noncommittal. "Zoned out," she said, but what did that mean?

Maggie seemed to think we were high on those brownies Laura brought to the Crones meeting, but I had just felt cheerful as I usually did in that group. People were being funny, yes, but they often were. I was going to find out what my buddies did to me when they were heated, not baked, and when I was alone.

I spread the pieces of the vaporizer on the kitchen table and stared at them. Which piece went where? What had the lass in the store said? How much bud went into the bulb? Did I light it first? Oh bugger, I thought, don't tell me you can't use it? What do you do when you need to know how to do something? Answer: the Internet.

On YouTube, a man on medicinal marijuana showed me how to use a vaporizer just like mine and I was off. The bud was supposed to be ground up in a grinder, but I didn't have one so I just crumpled it, pushed it into the bulb, prodded it down with a chopstick, and turned the machine on. When vapor appeared I sucked on the tube. All I got was a taste—no choking or coughing. I sucked again. And again.

This is no bloody good, I thought, it's not doing anything. I played carols and wrapped presents, taking a draw from the vaporizer every few minutes. Nothing happened, absolutely nowt. I had wasted my money.

The small Christmas tree in the living room looked good that year; its lights flickered in a fascinating rhythm—dim, then brighter, then even brighter—so bright they seemed to come at me. Funny, I didn't remember buying flashing lights. I thought they were just ordinary bulbs.

That dark bulb, the one with no color to it, and not flickering—I pulled up a chair and stared at it intently. Why wouldn't it light up? Why that bulb and not that one or that one? My stare became increasingly hostile. "Light up you bugger," I shouted. It didn't even wink back.

The other bulbs continued to brighten and fade. My head nodded as I followed them. Brighten and fade, brighten and fade, brighten and f-a-d-e, b-r-i-... The tree came closer and closer until the branches buried my head. My skin prickled as I rubbed my face on a branch giving the same sensation as a loofah.

"Loofah, loofah, stick it up your doodah," I carolled.

I drank in the smell of pine and closed my eyes to enjoy the sensation of flying through a pine forest, slowly at first and then faster and faster, air rushing past me, a whooshing sound, until I gasped with fright, opened my eyes, and took in the sight of my living room.

The Christmas tree glowed in one corner, my newly wrapped presents beneath it. Damn it, a bulb's gone.

22

IN FEBRUARY my third crop was still in veg, but almost ready to switch. The plants looked better than ever before, not only because they weren't battling spider mites, but also because I was a dab hand at pruning and I had started using tomato cages to hold them up. The last yield weighed in at over four pounds and I was hopeful that this one would reach five pounds. As this was the last crop under Marcus's supervision, I needed enough money to pay him back for the start-up expenses. Then I was on my own, though he had said he would still be there for me. At least, I think that's what he meant when he shuffled his feet and said, "I'll be around."

I emerged from the basement after a pruning session and was heading for the bathroom to wash and change when a knock came at the front door and a face pressed itself against the glass. It was too late to hide and as the face had seen me in the hall, I had to open the door.

Jason and Amy stood there knocking snow off their boots. "Hi, Mum," Jason said. "We hoped you'd be in. We've just left the kids to play with friends for an hour, so we thought we'd drop by for a cup of tea."

"Jason thought we should go to a café, but we haven't dropped in for a long time and we knew you'd be home," Amy said.

Should I tell them I had an infectious disease? That I was just on my way to the hospital? That I had an infestation of fleas? Instead I gave what I hoped was a welcoming smile. "Come on in. I'll put the kettle on." I headed for the kitchen and managed to at least wash my hands at the sink before they joined me.

"Let's sit in front of the fire," I said. "Go on in and I'll be with you in a jiff."

Amy, about to turn and leave for the living room, suddenly sniffed. She looked puzzled, but moved into the living room with Jason.

I took in the tea tray. "No baking, I'm afraid. Just some rather dull biscuits." I put the tray down. "So how are you all since I last saw you?"

There was an awkward silence as neither of them responded. Perhaps my discomfort at their presence showed?

"We've been talking about going to Mexico, to an all-inclusive. Get away from the snow and cold," Jason said.

"Everyone in Nelson dreams of going somewhere warm in February," I said. "Can you both get away from work?"

"I can, but Amy can't easily, can you?" Jason turned to Amy who had been sitting silent with a frown on her face.

Suddenly Amy sniffed again. And again. "I smell pot," she announced.

I glanced at Jason; his face was blank.

"Well, I don't smoke it," I said. "Must be from outside."

"No, not the smell of a joint," Amy said. "The smell of growing pot." She looked at me suspiciously. "I know that smell. I've had to rescue children from houses with grow-ops."

"I have been cooking," I said slowly. "Made soup with onions and herbs."

"It's more than that," Amy said. She sniffed with her nose held high.

I didn't know what to say or do. Jason stared out the window.

"You're growing pot," Amy said accusingly. She stood up and put her hands on her hips. "Look at you—you can't look me in the eye."

What could I say? Would it be better to firmly deny such an idea, or bluster? I chose the wrong option. "What I do in my house is my business," I said. "Now let's sit down and have a cup of tea."

"You're growing in the basement. Aren't you?" Amy stood up and glared down at me.

I stood up too. "Calm down, Amy. Maybe what you can smell is coming from the street." I could feel my pulse racing.

"No way. I'm going to check." Before I could stop her, Amy headed for the basement. I hadn't locked the door behind me like I usually do.

Jason and I stared at each other in horror. "I'm sorry, Mum. We should never have come, but Amy really wanted to." He jumped up.

"Let her go," I said as Jason headed for the basement. "She knows."

Furious thumps on the basement stairs and the slam of

the door announced the return of Amy. Jason and I stood rigid in the living room.

"She's got a grow-op down there. Can you believe it? And our children, her grandchildren, have been in this house." She strode up and down the living room, her face red and contorted and her chest heaving. "And Nicholas has been coming here regularly. I knew I shouldn't have let him." She turned to glare at me. "I'm going to phone the police."

Jason moved to face her. "No you're not," he said firmly. "You had no right to go down there without Mum's okay."

Amy stared at him in disbelief. "It's illegal to grow marijuana, as you well know. Your mother is a criminal and I'm going to report her." She marched out into the hall. "Jason, take me home."

Jason followed her and tried to put his arms round her. "Amy, come into the living room and we'll talk about this." He succeeded in leading her back.

Amy flung herself onto the living room couch. "I don't know how you can condone this, Jason. *You* might think it doesn't matter, but I do. What effect do you think it will have on our children? Your children?" She glared at her husband. "And I let Nicholas come here because you wanted me to."

"I am sure Mum didn't take him downstairs." Jason took a single chair, sat down leisurely and stretched out his legs. I silently handed out cups.

Amy, her face flushed and her voice strident, said, "You knew about this, Jason? You knew about it and did nothing?"

"No, I didn't know about it. I suspected, but I didn't know," Jason said calmly.

"And you still did nothing?"

"No." Jason took a sip of tea. "And I'm not going to do anything now. And neither are you."

"Oh yes, I am!" Amy spat the words out. "You don't expect me to let this pass without taking any action, do you? What if they find out at the office? I'll lose my job."

"Amy, you are not going to contact the police. No one need ever know and you are not going to tell anyone." Jason kept his voice even. "Not if you want our marriage to survive, that is."

Good for you, my baby boy. Take control, that's it. Be assertive. But don't threaten your marriage on my account.

"Don't you care about our children?" Amy yelled.

"Of course I care about our children," Jason said. "So does Mum."

"How could she? How could she *possibly* care about her grandchildren and still act like, act like…a fucking yardbird."

Amy glared at Jason as he replied, "Mum was put in a position of having no job and no income. She tried to get a job but the market is flat right now, and anyway it's hopeless for older people. So she started a business." He smiled at me. "I'm proud of her."

"She could have come and lived with us. We offered."

"Yes she could. And we did. But she is an independent old bat and will not be put under an obligation, to us or to anyone."

"Jason, it…is…illegal. I don't want our children growing up knowing their grandmother is a criminal," Amy said. She stood up and marched to the door. Then she turned around and glared at me. "And that friend of yours—Swan. The one who's looking after my children. Has she been helping you?

How else would you know what to do? Someone must be helping you. Is it Swan?"

I just stared at her. Should I boldly lie or tell her to bugger off?

"Is Swan helping you?" Amy repeated.

"It is none of our business," Jason said. "Amy, sit down and calm down."

Amy sat down again. "Do you want our children to grow up knowing their grandmother is a criminal?"

"There is no need for them to ever know," Jason said. "And if they do find out they'll have to come to terms with the fact that their father is a criminal too."

Amy's eyes widened. "Don't tell me you grow pot?"

"Not now. In my misspent youth. How do you think I afforded your engagement ring? I needed the money. As Mum does."

Amy stood up and rushed out of the room. I could hear her sobbing as she ran upstairs to the bathroom.

"Oh lordy," I said. "Jason, I can't bear to think that this will wreck your marriage. I'll stop, if you think it will help."

"No way, Mum. Amy should never have gone downstairs." He grinned. "Besides, it takes skill to grow pot. I think it's great that you even can."

"It's too bad that I'd just been pruning. The house doesn't usually smell. And the basement door is normally locked."

We both looked up as a red-eyed Amy entered the room. "I don't want you in my house, nor do I want you to have anything to do with my children," she said through clenched teeth.

Jason stood up and towered above her. "It is *our* house

and they are *our* children. Mum will continue to visit as always."

Amy glared up at him. "They are not coming here. No way."

"When they do come here," Jason said, emphasizing his words, "I am quite sure Mum will not take them down to the basement."

I shook my head. Jason continued. "You are going to forget this whole episode, Amy. You are going to forget that Mum grows. You are not going to dwell on it. I don't suppose she expects warmth from you when she visits on Sundays, but *I* expect civility to be shown my mother. Now, it's time to pick up the children."

As they put on their coats and boots in the hall, I said nothing. When Jason turned to hug me, I murmured, "I love you, my baby boy. Thank you for standing by me."

When I returned to the living room I was still trembling. I sat down, put my head back, and took deep breaths. The worst had happened—just what I had dreaded. Now what was I to do? There were really only two alternatives: stop or carry on. If I stopped I was more or less back to square one, with only social security to live on. That might be enough to keep me out of the food bank but not enough for any of the little pleasures of life and certainly not enough for a holiday in Yorkshire. I had always lived frugally, always counted pennies, always wondered how I would get through the month, and I was tired of it. I looked around and saw everyone else dressed by stores other than the thrift shops, eating out, driving cars without rust on them, using cell phones and laptops. Why not me?

If I carried on, it would be with the usual risk of getting caught and the additional risk of Amy informing on me anonymously. She might be too afraid of breaking up her marriage to do that, but how was I to know?

Oh bugger, now what was I going to do?

23

I SPENT MORE and more time on the computer. How I had ever lived without one? It was while I was in a shop that sold yarn that I learned of another use for it. I was looking for knitting patterns when the owner said, "We don't carry patterns any more. They're all online." I could search for patterns based on type of wool, which meant I could find ways of using up my collection of wool.

I discovered the games you could play too, and spent hours playing what I called Patience and they called Solitaire. But best of all I could write to Lisa and learn more about her life. She didn't seem to have any intention of ever living in Canada again, nor did she plan a holiday, but she did want me to visit her. The pictures she sent of the beaches near her and the tales of her work in Rotorua with the kiwi birds made me long to go.

Junk mail senders found me. One day I received an email with "Women love well-hung men" in the subject line. I opened it to find a colorful page asking if I was satisfied with the length, girth, and performance of my equipment. When it finally dawned on me what 'equipment' was, I cracked up and eagerly read on.

The ad extolled the virtues of Will-E-Up, a 'male enhancement' pill. This herbal product promised to increase the girth, the length, and the rigidity of my member leading to a harder erection and an enviable sex drive.

Testimonials followed: "My unit was small, soft, and droopy due to steroids. After two weeks on Will-E-Up, I am proud to present myself to my girlfriend."

"I am an older man. I have gained 2½ inches in length, and I am now 3¾ inches at the bore, and 9½ inches when hard. My wife is delighted. We are planning a second honeymoon."

"I am sixteen. Everyone used to point at my dick at school and laugh, but since I started taking Will-E-Up they now point at my Maestro of Mayhem wishing they had one like it."

Pictures of dejected penises raised to glory followed and all to be had for fifty dollars for one month's supply of pills or a hundred and forty-seven for a three-month supply of patches, patches to be applied to any part of the body for a few days at a time.

No doubt about it, there was much to be learned from the Internet.

It was while I was washing up that the idea occurred to me. Would my buds benefit if I gave them Will-E-Up? Would they become larger, harder, and erect? There was only one way to find out.

Life moved on. It felt great not to be constantly anxious about money. What a burden that is for people, wondering how to pay their bills, how to feed their kids, worrying about employment. Surely our wealthy society could do better than to tolerate the appalling percentage of children who grow up in poverty and have so many people without a home. And women of my age, women who have looked after everyone, raised families, been teachers and nurses and librarians—why should they end their days struggling to make ends meet? If I ran the universe it would not be like that. If governments followed the rule I grew up with—don't buy what you can't afford—we wouldn't be in this state.

I got over the showdown with Amy and the thought of packing it in. The fun I had had with my grow-op, the people I had met, people who cared about me like Swan and Maggie and even Marcus, the constant challenge and pleasure in my growing skills, the prospect of money—all these won out. I had changed from a nervous Nellie who couldn't tell a mari-juana plant from a chrysanthemum, to a competent indoor gardener. There was no way I was going to give it up.

I still had dinner with the family every Sunday. The first time after our showdown Amy was cold and silent, but it's hard to keep that up for long. It was Julie who rescued us. Over the last few months of her development she had turned into a right little chatterbox. As soon as I arrived at the door she hugged my legs and greeted me solemnly with her news.

"My milk went down the wrong way."

"Oh dear," I said. "Yes, that can happen."

She nodded her small, dark head. "But I'm okay."

Her speech was unbelievable for her age, and I delighted in her observations of life. "I thought a monster was coming to get me. I saw the monster. It was playing music."

"Wow. What did it look like?"

"It was this big," she said, stretching out her little arms. "With green hair and orange pants. But it's okay. It went away."

Jason became the stabilizing force. He and I had regained the closeness we enjoyed before he met Amy, and strangely, his marriage seemed to have improved after our debacle. Maybe Amy respected his assertive stand. Who knows what goes on between married couples?

After dinner one Sunday, Jason was upstairs dealing with a crisis in the children's lives: Blankie Bear was missing. At bedtime. No one could possibly settle for the night. Amy and I joined in the hunt downstairs and eventually he was located in the stroller.

I carried dirty dishes into the kitchen and helped Amy clean up. "How are you enjoying work?" I asked her.

"I think I liked being home more, to be perfectly honest. If Swan weren't so good with the kids, I would seriously think of quitting."

She had always been keen to go back to work, like so many married women, but the reality was not all roses.

"It's my case load that's so depressing," Amy continued. "Today, for example, I had a 65-year old woman, well educated, couldn't get a job, not eligible for welfare, who ended up literally sleeping in the park. Now she's in hospital with hypothermia." She stood up from stacking the dishwasher.

"The amount of money spent on treating her in hospital could have paid for housing for her. This government is—"

Amy was interrupted as Julie ran into the kitchen. "I just did a poo-poo in the potty," she said excitedly. "It was a mountain poo."

Both Amy and I expressed our delight at this news as we looked at each other and smiled.

A small packet, wrapped in plain brown paper, contained one month's supply of blue tablets in a blister package and a leaflet that promised satisfaction or my money back. Directions to take a daily dose, at bedtime, and to report unlikely side effects to the company were included on the insert. I popped out one pill to see if it would dissolve and to my delight, after a few minutes, it did.

My fourth crop, the first without Marcus, was planted and in its third week of veg. When should I administer the growth booster? I should set up an experiment. What was all that about Mendel and his separation of crops? He divided his land into different sections to try out different methods. If I did the same, the four lights were the obvious separators.

In the notebook I kept on my garden I wrote down:

Light One: nothing
Light Two: give pill three weeks into veg.
Light Three: give pill end of veg and beginning of bloom.
Light Four: give pill four weeks into flowering.

How many pills? I had no idea. One daily worked for a man, but one would not be enough for all the plants. I would try one for each plant so that would be eight for each light. Eight, dissolved in a watering can, would feed them when they were dry and could better absorb. They would only get one dose—after all, they were much smaller than a man.

What about the mothers? I'd better not experiment with them. If something went wrong, my future buddies would be lost. I could grow an extra mother next time and use that as a test case. Besides, the mothers didn't flower.

The eight plants under Light Two received their booster and I recorded this event on my calendar. I kept a file in the basement containing handouts from Michael, my notebook and a calendar that recorded waterings, feedings, harvest day, weight, and costs. I added a tape measure to my equipment to assess length of bud and—what was it?—bore.

I could hardly wait to visit the garden as soon as I got out of bed. Should I tell Maggie and Swan? If nothing happened I would look like an idiot. Better to wait and see.

My untroubled life was shattered when Maggie phoned one afternoon to see if I was home as she wanted to talk to me. She arrived looking anxious, quite unlike her usual serene self. We went into the kitchen and put the kettle on.

"Marcus has been arrested."

"What?" I had to sit down. Suddenly the enormity of what I was doing came back to haunt me. My basement life had become so ordinary that I never thought about the risks any more, and now reality's ugly face reared. "What for?" I managed to ask.

"He was building a room for a guy and the guy's friend called by and snitched on him. So the police came and found Marcus putting lights up."

"Surely that's not illegal?"

"No. And there were no plants around, thank god." Maggie stopped pacing and sat down across from me. "He was lucky. There's not much they can do. As you say it's not illegal to put lights in your house. It's the plants they want to see." She took a sip of tea. "The snitch was stupid. He should have waited until the plants were in and then informed the police. Can you believe a so-called friend would do that?"

"Yes, I can." I hadn't told Maggie about Amy finding me and I told her then. "So I'm never certain that she might not report me. She might if she had a row with Jason or something, but he made it pretty clear that their marriage would end if she did."

"Good for him." Maggie stretched her arms above her head. "God, with all the things wrong with the world, people make such an issue over a harmless weed. I can hardly believe it."

"Where is Marcus?"

"Still at the police station, I expect. I don't know what they'll charge him with. I think they took him in to frighten him and the guy he was working for. The trouble will be with Marcus's dad. I don't think his folks know what he does. Or," she added thoughtfully, "maybe they do but just ignore it. Marcus does do some legitimate electrical work as well, even though he hasn't got his ticket."

"Where does Marcus get his plants from if he doesn't grow himself? I've often wondered, but never got an answer out of him."

"He has quite a network. He's always setting people up like he did with you. He gets cuttings from them. Didn't he ever ask you for cuttings?" I shook my head.

I was about to tell her about my experiment but she got up to go. "I'll let you know what happens."

24

MAGGIE TOLD ME the next day that Marcus had not been charged and, after hanging around the police station for several hours, he'd been released. After that shock I'd found myself jumping when anyone came to the door, and I kept checking that the basement doors were locked. It was days before I settled down into my routine.

The crop grew and I watched it with eager anticipation. Would the buds be taller, harder, and fatter? The first notable difference was about five weeks into the flowering cycle, with three more weeks until harvest. Each day the test plants seemed jauntier. I began to use the tape measure to record their height and girth and sure enough, each day they gained a fraction of an inch in both. Lights Three and Four, which each got the booster when flowering were doing much better than Light Two, which got it in veg. In fact, it was hard to tell whether Light Two had benefited at all as there was so little difference between it and Light One, which got nothing.

I don't know when the buds began to change color as the process was so gradual, but one day they looked more purple than green—not a deep purple but with a sheen of greenish lavender. Bugger, was that healthy? Maybe I'd poisoned them. They might be bigger, but bigger isn't always better.

About two weeks before harvest, a light bulb didn't come on and I had to send for Marcus. I don't know what he'd been doing, but he showed up in frayed cut offs and smelling of the forest.

"Hi Marcus. A light won't go on." I had learned to stop babbling at him. Brief remarks seemed to elicit longer replies.

He did look at me before heading for the basement, but said nothing. He didn't even ask which light. I guess he would see that soon enough…why waste words?

He twisted the bulb in its socket. "Got a new bulb?"

I had just bought new bulbs, planning to replace them all at the start of the next crop. It was Light One that had gone out. He put in a new bulb but it still didn't come on.

"Turn it off," he said.

I turned off the ballast for that light and he produced a small screwdriver from his pocket and fiddled in the socket before putting the bulb back. "Now try."

The ballast hummed and the bulb glowed.

"Thank you," I said.

Marcus looked around and suddenly noticed the plants under Lights Three and Four, plants that extended their erect buds to the ceiling. His eyes widened. "Wow," he said. "What did you do?"

I smiled. "Fed them my special formula."

He bent down to examine a bud more closely. Then he

pinched it. "What formula?" He stood up and looked at me with the most animated expression I had ever seen on him. My plants had clearly excited him.

"I'll tell you after harvest," I said. "When I know if it works or not. Will you be here for my harvest?"

"Yep."

He took one last lingering look at the buds before leaving. "Hope they smoke," he muttered.

He left me with a horrible thought: what if the buds, large though they were, did not produce enough THC, or TLC as I called it, and were no good to smoke? Why hadn't I thought of that? But there was no sense in despair until I knew for sure. At least I had given it a try.

Harvest day arrived along with Swan and Maggie and their scissors. They didn't know where Marcus was, but thought he was in town—'tree planting' hadn't started yet. Candles burned all over the house, chairs and tables waited for the trimmers, and garbage bags and refreshments were at the ready. I didn't want Swan and Maggie to see my giant buds straight away so I had clipped the plants from Light One ready for them.

"You're on the ball," Maggie said.

"I'm always nervous on harvest day," I said. "Can't sleep. Don't know why." I did know why. It was the same anxiety exam sitters get wondering if they will succeed or fail.

Maggie and Swan began to trim and I made drinks before joining them. Swan worked with concentration and didn't say much. "What's up, Swan?" I asked her. "You look down in the dumps."

"My parents are on my case. Gotta go home." She snipped away at a bud, threw it in the box and picked up another plant. "This'll be my last trim."

"What are you going to do?" Maggie asked.

"Go to school."

"Is your two years up?"

Swan nodded. "Yeah. And my allowance."

"Allowance?" I was surprised. Was Swan a poor little rich girl? I had thought she was as strapped for cash as the rest of us.

Swan seemed to pick up my thought. "They've paid my rent. That's all."

"What are you going to study?" Maggie scraped leaves from her bin lid into the garbage bag.

Swan screwed up her face, shook her head from side to side, and answered, "Physics."

"Physics!" I stared at Swan with my mouth open.

She laughed when she saw the expression on my face. "You think I'm dumb, don't you? I aced it at school, especially in math. My dad teaches math."

I didn't think she was dumb, but I did think she was more, how shall I put it, artsy, more dreamy, more ethereal. Not the scientific type.

Maggie was equally surprised. "What in heaven's name are you doing in Nelson, waitressing and serving in a deli?"

Swan dipped her scissors in rubbing alcohol, wiped them on a towel, and didn't reply. She was close to crying. Poor kid. I felt sorry for her even though I couldn't relate to her experience. I left school and went to work in a mill for a year until I was old enough to start nurse training in a hospital. There was no prospect of travel or taking a break and an allowance was out of the question.

Maggie looked up from her plant. "I've taken a few college courses but not physics, that's for sure. So, you're going back to California, Swan?"

"Yes. In two weeks. I'm enrolled at Berkeley. Starting September."

"Are you looking forward to it?" Maggie asked.

"I suppose," Swan said. She hesitated. "I want to go to school. It's living at home that's brutal."

"Can't you live in a dorm? Tell your folks that you can work better living on campus. No commuting. Save time."

"Our house is practically on campus." Swan thought for a moment. "But that's a great idea. I'll tell them I need to work in the labs in the evenings if I want good grades. They won't like the idea of my coming home late at night." She stared at her bud, clipped one small leaf off it and threw it into the box.

"We shall miss you," I said and meant it. I had known she would be leaving eventually, but the time to face up to it had arrived. Right then, I was too excited at the prospect of their amazement when they saw my giant buds. I would do my grieving later.

We finished Lights One and Two and broke for lunch. When we returned Maggie and Swan settled in their chairs and I went to clip the first of my wondrous plants. I carried them in as casually as I could and their astonishment was just as I had hoped.

"Holy Shit, *what* are those?" Maggie said, leaning forward to pick up a plant.

Swan's eyes opened wide. "Did you put them on steroids?"

"Are they another variety?" Maggie asked.

"No, same old Jamaican." I tried not to smirk. "I fed them a special formula." I hadn't meant to tell them what formula, but I couldn't keep quiet. "I gave them penis enhancers."

"You're kidding!" Swan said and they both cracked up. "Penis enhancers?" She picked up a bud and stroked its length. "I don't believe it."

"I knew a man whose wife told him to get a penis enhancer," Maggie said. "He did. She was twenty-four and her name was Tiffany."

We were all hysterical by this time and when we calmed down we began to trim the mighty buds.

"This isn't going to take long," Maggie said. "There are only a few of them." She hefted one. "They're really heavy."

Swan held a bud under the light and peered at it. "They're a funny color. Purplish."

"Yes, I wonder if I've poisoned them." I picked up a bud, at least twelve inches long and so thick my hand barely circled it. "My big worry is whether they're smokeable."

"I hadn't thought of that," Maggie said.

"If they're not, then they're no good, beautiful though they may be."

"We won't know until Marcus tries to sell them. Then he'll either arrive with mega-bucks or I'll just get money for those," I said, indicating the hanging buds we'd trimmed earlier.

"I want to be here when he comes back from the seller," Maggie said.

"Let's have a party to say good-bye to Swan and to either celebrate or drown our woes," I said.

We set a date for a week later; Maggie would bring her scale in the morning and we'd have the party the following evening, Swan's last night. Swan said she would make sure Marcus was up to speed and could make our date.

That was the beginning of a period of ear-pulling anxiety. Either I had ruined half the crop and would only get money for two pounds or else I had created wonder buds and would reap riches.

To get ready for the party, I went shopping for clothes—and not in a thrift shop. Some snazzy jeans with a sort of cut-out pattern down the leg hung in the petite section of a real clothing store. When I first saw them I thought they'd be draughty but then, what the hell, I tried them on. They fit perfectly and I didn't have to cut off the bottoms. The older woman serving said, "Those look good on you," and I bought them. Then I found some "stick on" tattoos and I bought a pair that went around your ankles, like bracelets. Right trendy I was.

It took a week for my Big Buddies to dry. I examined them every day willing them to dehydrate so they'd be ready and sold before Swan left. A heater and a fan helped, but I was still doubtful when Maggie arrived to weigh them.

"I'm not sure if they're dry," I said. "They've hardly shrunk and they're too big to see if a stalk snaps."

"It's been a week hasn't it? They should be okay by now. Let's go ahead."

As usual, Maggie weighed a plastic bag and then she reverently placed a Big Buddy on the scale. One alone weighed more than four ounces and two came to over the required eight ounces per bag.

"What do we do here?" Maggie said. "I don't want to break them to make exactly half a pound and we can't add the other little ones."

"Let's just put two buds in each bag and if they weigh more, so what?" I said.

We tried to match a bigger bud with a smaller one, but there were no smaller ones. Each of the two lights had produced thirty-two buds, four per plant, so in the end we had sixty-four buds weighing more than sixteen pounds.

"Holy Shit," Maggie said. "Sixteen pounds at two thousand a pound is thirty-two thousand! You'll be rich."

"That's only two lights. With four, there'd be twice that amount."

We stared at each other in amazed delight. Then I remembered. "They might not be smokeable."

"When's Marcus showing up?"

"Some time today, I hope," I said. "Hey, don't let's forget the other buds."

With a decided lack of enthusiasm we weighed and packed the regular buds from Lights One and Two. They came to a puny two and a half pounds. Normally, I would have been delighted but my perspective had changed. What was five thousand dollars when you could make thirty-two?

Pride cometh before a fall, I could hear my mother saying and the fall here could be more than a tumble. If the Big Buddies were impotent, they would be worthless. I would still make five grand but I would have wasted the crop from two lights. On the other hand, the experiment had been fun even if it didn't pay off.

Marcus arrived that morning while Maggie was still there. "You won't believe what Jess has done," she said to him. "Sixteen pounds off two lights! These half-pound bags weigh more than they should because we can't split the buds."

"Hope they smoke," Marcus said as he stashed the bags.

"Are there buyers in town?"

"Yep. Should know soon."

"We'll see you tomorrow evening then?" I said.

"Yep."

I don't know how I got through the time until we all met and Marcus would give the verdict. It was like playing one of those television games where, if you guess right you win something large, but if you're wrong you get nothing. I wouldn't end up with nothing of course—the small buddies would still earn me five thousand dollars, a not insignificant sum. But if the big buddies were potent….

I repeated thirty-two thousand over and over to myself. What would I do with it? Go and see Lisa for one thing. Help out some of the crones for another. I would tell them I'd received the inheritance I'd mentioned and that I wanted to share it. They wouldn't accept money, but I could arrange for us all to go on a cruise, a cruise to Alaska or Hawaii, on a luxury liner, with deck cabins, chaise longues spread out invitingly by the emerald pool, martinis in the sunset, young men waiting on us. When I got to figuring out how much that would cost, thirty-two thousand dollars wouldn't be nearly enough. Besides, when everyone struggled to make ends meet every month, it was a waste of money to spend so much on a few days luxury—supermarket gift certificates would make more sense.

I thought about Ed and Eva. I could pay for a decent nursing home for Eva. The thought thrilled me. How would I do it anonymously? Through some foundation? I would have to find out. And Marcus. I could help send him to the Mayo Clinic or wherever his parents wanted. I just needed to figure out a way of hiding how I'd got the money and of no one knowing who had paid.

Fortunately, cleaning the basement, filling plant pots with fresh soil and planting the seedlings in them, kept me physically busy, but my mind wouldn't let up. If I gave Will-E-Up to all the plants in the flowering stage, and if they all responded, then there would be one hundred and twenty-eight giant buds to harvest. If they weighed the same as the trial bunch, I would earn sixty-four thousand per crop. Then what would I do? Not invest it, that was for sure.

Would I quit? Twenty more grows would make me a millionaire. I laughed at the thought. Me, Jess, a waitress, a millionaire? It wouldn't all fit under my mattress.

Then I became obsessed with the idea of buying Bob's Café and starting a business. I could employ all the Crones and open a teashop. If there's one thing older women know how to do, it's make date squares and cakes. We could sell them in the teashop. And if we worked short shifts, say two hours, everyone could earn money serving.

By the time Swan and Maggie arrived for our party, I was a nervous wreck. I had rescued Ceres from the basement and hung her over a bottle of champagne like an Olympic medal. We left it in the fridge for when Marcus arrived and started on a pleasant white wine, while the stuffed chicken breasts cooked on the barbecue.

"Are you all packed, Swan?" Maggie asked her.

"Uh huh. Leave first thing." Swan waved at Elephant Mountain. "I'm going to miss all this."

"You can always come back for a holiday," I said. "I have a spare bed."

"Are you flying out?" Maggie asked.

"Got a ride down with some guys going to San Francisco. Dad will pick me up from there." Swan looked anything but thrilled as she spoke.

In a way I felt sorry for her, but why feel sorry for someone about to go to university and begin her life? She'd had her playtime. I didn't want to think about my life without her, and anyway at that moment I was too wound up waiting for Marcus.

We held dinner and drank more wine until he came. Finally his truck pulled up at the back and he ambled into the basement. I rushed to unlock the inside basement door.

Marcus joined us on the balcony. Maggie and Swan got up and we all stood there with expectant looks on our faces, like a Victorian tableau.

Marcus looked at us with his usual expressionless stare. He held what seemed to be a very full garbage bag.

"Oh come on, Marcus," Maggie said. "Were they smokeable?"

"Yep."

"Were you able to sell them?" I asked.

"Yep."

"Tell us, Marcus. What did they say?" Maggie urged him as she handed him a glass of wine.

"Awesome buds. Great smoke."

"How much did you get?"

Marcus sipped at his wine and looked at us all with an expressionless face. Then he grinned. "Three thousand a pound."

"What!" I turned to Maggie and Swan and we hugged each other and laughed. I couldn't believe it. With the little buddies thrown in that would be over fifty thousand dollars. I could be a millionaire after only ten more grows. In less than three years!

Marcus handed over the garbage bag. I glanced into it and at the bundles of hundred dollar bills. It was all I could do to stop myself opening one and tossing bills all over the balcony. I was rich. No more food banks. No more servility. No more money worries. Holidays were for me. I did deserve them. I was a champion.

I could help the Crones and Eva and Marcus. Marcus. I gave him a big hug, which he endured, but didn't return. I had learned to love him as he was, so I wasn't sure about helping him seek treatment, but that was a thought for another day. Having shared my formula with Maggie, she would be able to grow huge buds too and would be able to go to school soon. The food bank would get a massive anonymous donation. And I would—

"Time for champagne," Maggie said.

Marcus opened the bottle and we cheered at that satisfying plop of the released cork. We raised our glasses to each other.

"Bon voyage, Swan," I said.

"Here's to Mary Jane," Marcus said.

"And here's to the darling buds of Jess."

25

A YEAR LATER, Granny's Garden opened. Buying the business from Bob and then leasing the premises and getting a business licence had all been easy, even though I'd never done anything like that before.

My plan was to open the place as a teashop and have the Crones bake for it, for money of course. And if any of them wanted to serve, they could do that too.

We were having our usual meeting when I brought up the idea. "I've inherited some money," I said, "and I want to open a café. A teashop. What do you think?"

"People don't drink tea," Jane said. "Why not a coffee shop?"

"There are coffee shops on every block in Nelson. This will be different."

"I'll come," Nina said. "I love tea."

"What will you serve besides tea?" Laura asked.

"That's what I was getting to. How would you all like to bake and earn a bit of money. Joan makes those delicious muffins, for example, and you all have a specialty."

The group went silent as everyone thought about it.

"I'm not sure if I have the energy to bake every day," Fran said.

"Oh, it wouldn't be every day," I said. "You could bake whenever you wanted to. But on a regular basis. Say every Tuesday or something."

"We could always freeze batches," Maggie said. "Most baked goods freeze well. Then we could bake when we felt like it." She looked around and then turned to me. "I assume we'll be baking there? In the café's kitchen?"

I nodded.

"Oh what fun!" someone said.

More silence. Then, "Will you have mixers and blenders? It's really easy to make dough in those big mixers."

"I haven't fixed up the kitchen yet, but I plan on making it easy to bake in and with all the mod cons."

The existing kitchen would do, but it was too crummy for my café. My café was going to have easy-to-reach ovens, a large central work table with electric outlets for mixers, and big sinks. Everything stainless steel. Like in a magazine.

People were beginning to sit up and look interested.

"I could do date squares like my mother used to make," Fran said.

"Yes," Claire said, "and I used to get Women's Institute ribbons for my chocolate cake."

"Did you really?" Claire was always full of surprises.

"Perhaps I could make Craig's brownies," Laura said. "If he'll give me the recipe. He said it was a secret recipe, but if I tell him it's all for a good cause he might."

Maggie and I exchanged glances.

Everyone began to talk at once, enthusiastically recalling the baking they had done as housewives.

"We'll have to have real ingredients," Maggie said. "No mixes or the crap they make now. Do you know how to source?"

"Sauce? You mean make gravy?" I asked.

Maggie laughed. "No. Source—locate and buy supplies."

"Haven't a clue," I said. "How would you like to manage that?"

Maggie nodded. "Sure. I've learned a lot at the Co-op."

"Everyone will get paid of course." I hadn't worked out how much, but certainly more than minimum wage. Say, twice minimum wage. Would giving up the garden be possible? Three or four more crops would take care of the lease for at least two years and cover other costs. After that, would my takings be enough? I could always reduce the number of plants but if I was going to grow at all, it was a waste not to grow a whole room. Did I really want to give it up? It was work, yes, but work I enjoyed and there was something satisfying about producing my giant buds.

"When do we start?" Fran asked.

"There's still a lot to do before we open. I've only just leased the place and it's a dump. Dark green paint and plastic tablecloths. It's going to be bright and cheery and I want it to look like a garden even though it's inside. You can all come and see it when there's something to see."

"I don't bake," Thelma said. "So I guess I'm out of it."

"There'll be lots of other things to do, especially when it comes to designing the place." I smiled at her. "There's work for everybody."

"I used to help with set design," Thelma said. "I wonder if I can still draw a plan."

After that everyone talked at once, full of ideas and I wished I'd had a notebook to write some of them down. The Stitch and Bitch group got into how they could make doilies and embroidered napkins like a proper teashop. I didn't like to tell them I hated doilies. My mother used to think they were a frippery nonsense, and that was one of the few things we agreed on.

Maggie put paid to the napkins idea by asking me if I intended to have a washing machine. I hadn't thought of that.

Then I had the fun of designing the place like an English country garden. I wanted lots of flowers, especially climbing ones. They would have to be artificial of course, but there were classy silk ones to be had that looked real. This is where Thelma came into her own. She took measurements and in a few days presented me with a professionally drawn plan. Boxes of climbing roses, violets, pansies, and foxgloves separated the space into little arbors that held rustic tables and chairs.

"It looks wonderful, Thelma. I love the idea of arbors, but we do need to be able to serve. This one," I said pointing, "has no entrance. We need a clear path from the kitchen to each table."

"Right," she said cheerfully. "I hadn't thought of that. Easy to re-do."

A couple of days later Thelma produced the design that we finally used. I gave her a check for two hundred and fifty dollars and she nearly fell over. "That's too much," she gasped.

"No it's not. I've used your skills and I'm grateful for

them. I had no idea you could do something like this. Now, give me some suggestions for the boxes and I'll see about getting them made."

At home it was harvest time. Marcus and Maggie came to trim and by then I was also pretty good. With my usual huge buds we were finished by lunchtime and we sat down to enjoy one of Maggie's casseroles.

"What's happening with the café?" Maggie asked.

"Thelma's come up with a lovely design. Looks like an English garden with lots of flowers. Here, I'll show you." I fetched the plan and Maggie studied it.

Marcus sat there munching, not paying any attention.

"Look Marcus." Maggie pushed the paper where he could see it. "What do you think?"

He stared at the plan. Then he picked up his fork again and said, "Needs lights."

"Where would you put them?" Would Marcus help? My eyes lit up at the thought.

He glanced at the plan again. "Here, here, here." He pointed to each arbor.

"Would you do that?" I asked him. "I'd pay of course."

"Yep."

"Now all I need is someone with carpentry skills who can make the flower boxes and trellises," I said. "Do you know anyone?"

"Marcus can do that," Maggie said. "He can turn his hand to anything, can't you?"

"Yep."

"Okay. Order what you need and give me the bill. Have you got the right tools?" I remembered Swan saying he was a—what did she call it?—MacGyver, but I'd never needed his services other than in the garden.

And so Marcus spent a few days at the café building the flower boxes and the trellises. Once I'd got used to the idea that he would never ask me what I wanted, I just let him get on with it. The boxes were beautifully finished—cedar, rectangular with a smooth rim, and interwoven GG letters carved in the front. When they were finished I arranged for him and Thelma to come to the café to set them up.

Thelma breezed in dressed as if for a royal garden party in high-heeled shoes and an enormous black straw hat with grapes and leaves around the crown.

"Oh you must be Marcus," she gushed. "I've heard so much about you."

Marcus tried to back away, but Thelma held out a gloved hand and when he didn't come forward, she took hold of his hand in both of hers and held it a moment too long. "Don't be shy, darling. Come and sit down so we can get to know one another." She looked around, but there was nowhere to sit. "Never mind, we'll go for coffee when our work's done."

Marcus looked like a frightened rabbit, but the pile of flower boxes and trellises blocked his escape.

Thelma took off her hat and gloves. "Now to work. Marcus, you put the boxes where I show you and Jess, you hold the tape measure. When do the flowers arrive?"

"I've ordered them and they should be here next week."

"Good. Now Marcus, use those strong, manly arms to

put this box right here." She pointed at the spot and he hastily moved the box.

With Thelma organizing us, we soon had the boxes arranged and the trellises fixed up. Marcus came back the next day and installed concealed lighting in each arbor and after the flowers went in the result was like fairy grotto. I drew up a chair to gaze around. My café. I hugged myself. My café that would support me and the Crones in our old age.

A Public Health inspector visited and approved my plan for a new kitchen so I called in a contractor to get on with it. I didn't care how much it cost as long as I got what I wanted.

After the wrought-iron tables and cushioned chairs arrived, the Crones came to take a look. I made tea and served it with the muffins I had ordered from Joan. It wasn't our usual meeting and as everyone was divided into small groups in the arbors, I couldn't ask them as a group what they thought. However, the lively chatter and laughter told me they liked the place.

Most of them were keen to be waitresses as long as the shifts were no longer than four hours, but none of them had ever done the job before. Nina was too frail to serve and she didn't bake. What job could I find for her? Design the menus maybe.

I gathered the willing waitresses together for their first lesson—how to set a table. "You must be careful to keep your hands away from the cakes and you only handle cups by the handles," I said.

The group was unimpressed. "I always put the fork on the right when I set my table," Fran said.

"Oh, I don't. I put mine on the left. With the napkin."

"Shouldn't it be on the plate? That means in the middle."

"No, the plate goes on the left."

"Look," I said, "I don't care where you put the fork. Just don't touch the tines."

Was this what my workforce was going to be like? I hadn't even begun on how to serve. Maybe I should hire a couple of youngsters too? They would give stability if a Crone decided not to show up, or if someone got tired. But then it wouldn't be a place run entirely by older women.

"I think we should wrap the forks in the napkins, don't you Jess? That way they'll stay clean," Maggie said.

"Good idea."

I was back in the kitchen when Laura breezed in waving a piece of paper. "Craig gave me the recipe," she said triumphantly, "but I can't make out the name of the special herb. Anyway, here it is."

Medicinal Brownies
½ cup butter
4 squares (1oz/30g) unsweetened chocolate
4 eggs at room temperature
½ tsp salt
2 cups sugar
1 tsp vanilla
1 cup flour
1 cup slivered almonds
1/3 cup browned (word indecipherable)

"I still don't know exactly what the herb is," Laura said, "and I can't read this."

"Let's ask Maggie," I said and went to fetch her.

"Here's the recipe for my brownies." Laura handed the paper to Maggie, "but I don't know what the herb is. I think he said 'kif.' Do you know?"

"Yes. It's difficult to get hold of, but I do know of a source." Maggie smiled.

"That's great, Laura," I said. "I'm sure they'll be very popular. But I think we'll call them Granny's Garden Brownies not Medicinal."

"Good idea. But as these brownies do have a medicinal compound, I think we should limit them to one per customer," Maggie said.

After Laura had left the kitchen I said to Maggie, "What if someone, like the police, comes in and finds the 'medicinal compound' in the kitchen? What do we do?"

"Don't worry. You or I can store it at home and bring it in as needed. And we'll add grated zucchini to explain the green bits." Maggie thought for a moment. "And I don't think we should advertise them openly."

"How would people know they're on the menu?"

"Word would soon get around."

"No. Then it becomes subterfuge. I think we should just have them on the menu, but limit them. Most people won't realize they are different anyway."

The Grand Opening occurred one Friday in early fall. A huge bouquet of real flowers arrived from Swan and a note simply saying, "Gluck" with a happy face. All the Crones were on board, dressed in frilly, embroidered aprons. These had satisfied the sewing group, and the laundry problem, as the aprons were individually owned and taken home to wash. We decided on paper napkins of good quality with a design of bright red field poppies.

Thelma, the official Hostess, outfitted in a long, mauve Edwardian dress that clung to her slim figure, a matching wide-brimmed hat trimmed with purple voile, and purple gloves, met people at the door and led them to a table.

"How charming to see you," she said. "What a beautiful day to enjoy a cup of tea and a homemade cake. Here is our list of teas and tempting confections." She handed over a menu with a gracious sweep of her arm. "We do have coffee if you wish. Your server will be with you shortly."

Jason and Amy came on opening day and this time I was thrilled to be able to serve Amy. Jason gave me a giant hug. "I'm so proud of you, Mum. Owning your own café yet!"

Amy looked around. "Jess, this is amazing! Such a change from the usual. I'm not sure about the carbohydrate overload, but what a treat." She looked at the menu. "What shall we have, Jason? I think I'd like a date square."

"Mmm, a brownie for me, I think."

I served them tea and a plate of cakes and left them to it. When I went back, Amy gave me a huge smile and said, "Those brownies are the best I've ever tasted."

With shaking shoulders, Jason bent over to retrieve his napkin from the floor and then sat up to give me a nudge.

"Made with real, local ingredients," I said, "and baked by a master baker."

I had invited Marcus, but didn't expect him to come. However, he appeared and hung around in the doorway looking ready to back out when Thelma rushed up to him and said, "Darling, I'm so glad you could come. You must sit here at this table reserved for very special guests." She led him to an arbor at the back and sat down with him. As I appeared to serve she was saying, "Of course tea is on the house. Or would you prefer coffee? And which of these mouth-watering delicacies takes your fancy?"

Marcus, silent as always, studied the menu.

Thelma looked up at me and said, "I'll take a break now, Jess, and sit with Marcus. After all the work he did here, he is our honored guest, is he not?" She laid her hand on his arm.

I kept an eye on them as I served. I might have needed to rescue Marcus, but although Thelma did all the talking in her demonstrative way, he contentedly munched on at least six cakes and ignored her.

Initially we attracted older customers who responded by sitting up straight and unfolding a napkin over their laps as if they were taking tea in a stately home. They seemed to enjoy the date squares and Claire's chocolate cake the most, and would often have second servings.

I listened in to reminiscences of the cakes they ate as children:

"I haven't had chocolate cake like this since my mother died."

"This tart is better than the ones Gran baked. I wonder if they do Yorkshire parkin?"

That was a thought. I used to make parkin. I had enough on with running the place to be baking as well, but maybe I could teach one of the others.

I didn't think our café would appeal to young customers, but not long after we opened a teenager with long curly hair came in accompanied by a replica of Swan. They glanced around and as Thelma approached, he quickly turned to the door, but the girl stopped him and whispered something. Thelma seated them and I brought them menus.

When I showed them the list of cakes the girl asked, "What's a Granny's Garden Brownie?"

"It's a brownie with a special herb that older people find helps their arthritis," I said. "But younger people also seem to like them."

"We'll have two, please," the girl said. "And a pot of black tea."

As I served them I wondered how they would respond to what was clearly a new experience for them. They probably thought a teashop run by old biddies was weird, something to laugh about with their friends.

"What the f…, *what* is that?" the boy said pointing at the teapot.

"It's a tea cozy. Keeps the tea warm."

The girl fingered it. "Did someone knit this? My gran had one like it. Years ago."

"They still work," I said and left them to it.

After a while, they called me over. With a big smile the girl said, "We'd like two more brownies please."

"I'm sorry," I said, "our policy is to restrict them to one per customer because they are so difficult to make."

"Right. Let's have something else, Rob." She studied the menu. "I'd like chocolate cake and a meringue. How about you?"

He nodded. I took them the cakes. They dug into them as if they had never eaten cakes before.

"We'll be back," the girl said as she paid the bill. "Your cakes are yummy."

And they did return. Along with their friends.

After three months Granny's Garden was so busy I had to hire kitchen help for the Crones. They continued to bake, but a couple of youngsters helped them with the menial tasks like washing up and taking trays out of the oven. Granny's Garden Brownies were by far the most popular item on the menu, particularly with young people, some of whom became regulars. Thelma and I got much pleasure from chatting to them about their lives and their ambitions and over time, we became a sort of advisor to some—Agony Grannies, if you like.

The customers who gave me the greatest thrill were Ed and Eva. Through a lawyer I had been able to pay for a room for Eva in a private nursing home in Nelson without Ed finding out. He'd been told that a trust fund that helped former loggers paid, and he accepted that.

Once Eva was settled in her new home, he brought her to the café one morning for a Crones meeting, before we opened to the public. All the Crones came, brownies were served and we had a meeting.

"It gives me much pleasure," I said, "to welcome Eva back to Nelson and to our cooperative café, which, as we all know, has added so much to the local scene."

The Crones applauded.

Eva looked around with a genuine smile. Then she reached for Ed's hand and in a surprisingly strong voice sang, "Hold my hand, it's a garden in Paradise. Lost in a wonderland…"

All the Crones joined in and then someone started on Ta-ra-ra Boom-de-ay. Thelma jumped up and danced around each table singing:

"Ta-ra-ra Boom-de-ay
I went to church today
I heard the parson say
Ta-ra-ra Boom-de-ay."

She thrust her bum out at every Boom and collapsed on a chair, breathless. Then they all got up and began to polka. Oh God, someone was sure to have a heart attack. How could I calm them down? Did I need to? What's wrong with older women having a good time?

Finally they all flopped, laughing, onto chairs. Someone said, "Is there anything else to eat?" and that set them off again.

One day we were busy with American tourists visiting Nelson during spring break. They were some of our best customers. My café brought out reminiscences of visits to the Old Country and Devon cream teas and pubs, and they were very generous tippers. A smart young woman in designer jeans and a tailored jacket walked in and stood looking around. I bustled out of the kitchen to seat her. "Hi Jess," she said.

My eyes widened. "Swan!" I hugged her. "Oh Swan. It is

so good to see you." Tears welled up. "Let me look at you." I held her away from me. "You look so…so, what? Professional. How are you? Come and sit down. How long are you here for?" I dragged her to a table.

"So what's with this? Have you become an honest woman? Hey, are those the same loafers?" She looked at my feet.

"These? Oh these are the latest in comfort. And not from the thrift shop, I can tell you."

Swan sat down and stretched out her legs. She picked up one of Nina's hand-painted menus. "Is this what you sell here? A high-carb fix?"

"You should try the brownies. They're our favorite. I'll get you one with some tea." I rushed to the kitchen and asked Fran if she would mind serving us as I had a special friend come into town.

"It's coming," I said as I sat down. "Now tell me what you're doing and how you are."

She looked quite different from how I remembered her. Less flakey, more serious, studious almost. No makeup at all and her beautiful eyes shone with health…and what? Serenity? Peacefulness? She really was a picture.

"I'm only here for a quick visit, on my way to Vancouver from Spokane. With my family. They came this way for me because I so badly wanted to see you." She smiled. "I've been dying to see your new business." She looked up at the climbing flowers. "Sweet."

Fran arrived and set down a teapot, crockery, and two brownies on a plate. "Try one of our famous brownies," I said as I pushed the plate toward Swan.

She took a bite, stared at me, nodded, and said with

a laugh, "What's in them? As if I can't guess. Are you still growing?"

"I'm hoping to stop if we make enough money here. Trouble is, I enjoy growing. And I'm still getting great results."

"You could cut down. Say to one light. Is Marcus still around?" She finished her brownie and licked her lips.

"He comes to fix things if I need him and carries in soil for me—that sort of thing. He's just the same. He and Maggie trim. Maggie leaves this summer to go to school. Anyway, if I do cut down, I can trim by myself. But I want to know about you."

Swan told me about her program. She was acing it, she hung out with a gang rather than have one BF, she lived in a dorm on campus, her parents were less of a pain, and she missed Nelson. "I'll always look back on my time here as the best years of my life. I was so free. I met such cool people. You, for one."

Me? Cool?

"Tell me what your real name is. I know it isn't Swan, is it?"

"Nah." She smiled. "But I'll always be Swan to you."

I saw her to the door and stood there watching her walk down the street, toward the burnt-out restaurant where we had worked together. What would have happened to me if I hadn't met her? She had changed my life. I would probably have ended up as a built-in baby sitter for Jason and Amy in their sterile house. I laughed. Well, bugger that for a lark!

Acknowledgments

Writers cannot write seriously without the help of many others. My grateful thanks go to:

My brilliant and insightful writing group who always give me stimulating suggestions and ideas—Vangie Bergum, Jane Byers, Sarah Butler, Anne deGrace, Rita Moir, Kristene Perron, and Verna Relkoff.

The city of Nelson, BC for its unique community.

Three skilled growers who generously shared their time and knowledge.

The memory of my Auntie Von, a feisty Yorkshire woman on whom Jess is based and who taught me so much.

All the cheerful help and enthusiasm from Second Story Press.

About the Author

JENNIFER CRAIG became a nurse in the UK shortly after WWII and immigrated to Canada in the 1960s. During her midlife crisis, she obtained a Bachelor's degree in nursing, followed by a Master's in education and a Ph.D. in medical education from McGill. She was on the Faculty of Medicine at UBC for ten years as an educational consultant. She is the author of the memoir *Yes Sister, No Sister: My Life as a Trainee Nurse in 1950s Yorkshire*, which sold more than 160,000 copies in the UK. She lives in Nelson, BC.